THE HAPPY-GO-L

Edward Thomas's only novel ~~has~~ ~~much~~ ~~of~~ ~~auto~~-biography in it. Far from being a novel in the orthodox sense, with a plot which unfolds in an orderly fashion, it is an evocation of a time and a place and a group of characters, one of those summings-up of a particular atmosphere at which Thomas excelled. The Morgans live untidily in a large house in a neat road in Balham, on the edge of London; as well as the family, there is the faithful servant Ann and a galaxy of hangers-on. Wales forms a constant spiritual background to the Morgans' existence, and many of the conversations and stories are about their distant homeland, stories told with all the poet's skill. There is a constant tension between impractical reality—Mr Morgan never works and seems always to be on the verge of bankruptcy, yet the impending disaster never comes—and the practical but far less real world outside. Eventually, after a magical spring, Philip Morgan, the narrator's companion, dies, and the family return to Wales, leaving only 'dim hazed spirits of men and children, dogs and pigeons', ruled by 'a haze of ghostly, shimmering silver'.

THE HAPPY-GO-LUCKY MORGANS

Edward Thomas

Introduction by Glen Cavaliero

THE BOYDELL PRESS

Introduction © 1983 Glen Cavaliero

First published in BOOKMASTERS 1983
by The Boydell Press
an imprint of Boydell and Brewer Ltd
PO Box 9, Woodbridge, Suffolk, IP12 3DF

British Library Cataloguing in Publication Data.
Thomas, Edward
The happy-go-lucky Morgans.
I. Title
823'.8[F]   PR6039.H55

ISBN 0 85115 223 6

Printed in Great Britain by
St Edmundsbury Press, Bury St Edmunds, Suffolk

INTRODUCTION

The Happy-Go-Lucky Morgans is Edward Thomas's only novel—if novel one may call it when he himself was reluctant to do so. On a first reading it seems a rag-bag of a book, an inconsequential collection of stories, sketches, reminiscence, and elaborate portrayals of landscape; which is why, possibly, it has hitherto not been reprinted. A book hard to classify, it is one of the author's most revealing works, valuable not only as autobiography but also, though less obviously, as an experiment in the art of fiction. Its neglect has done Edward Thomas a disservice.

The book has, however, been admired by several of his critics. If John Moore in describing it as 'a queer, delightful, nondescript thing' may sound a shade dismissive, Harry Coombes, a rigorous and perceptive commentator, remarks that 'Despite some lapses into triviality it is one of the most delightful and best sustained of Thomas's prose books', a verdict which its readers are likely to endorse. The novel has great immediacy, an immediacy springing from its roots in the author's inner life: as much as the posthumously published *Childhood of Edward Thomas* (1938) it helps one to understand the man behind the poems. As W. H. Hudson noted in a letter to Edward Garnett, 'every person described in it . . . are one and all just Edward Thomas,' percipiently adding that 'A poet trying to write prose fiction often does this.'

The novel's autobiographical nature may have arisen from the fact that it was one of the few uncommissioned books that Thomas wrote. His own opinion of his literary career may be deduced from his account here of 'Mr Torrance', who 'wrote what he was both reluctant and incompetent to write, at the request of a firm of publishers whose ambition was to have a bad, but nice-looking, book on everything and everybody, written by some young university man with private means, by some vegetarian spinster, or a doomed hack like Mr Torrance.'

But *The Happy-Go-Lucky Morgans* was composed in a desultory manner to please Thomas himself; and the intermittent nature of its evolution, perhaps in part owing to the fact that, as Moore suggests, he 'had got out of the habit of writing except to order', allowed the book to grow as a poem grows. Its importance for Thomas's literary development may lie in the fact that in it he could sift and examine his own romanticism, unconsciously working towards the steady and comprehensive perspective of the poems.

Although not directly autobiographical, the book evokes the world of South London as it was in the time of Thomas's Wandsworth boyhood. This was an area known also to E. M. Forster, for the original of 'the Wilderness' which adjoins the Morgan house (the name is a pleasing coincidence) once formed part of the grounds of Battersea Rise, the girlhood home of Forster's great-aunt, Marianne Thornton. Like Abercorran House it was demolished and built over. (Abercorran House itself was modelled on one inhabited by relatives of the Welsh poet, Lewis Morris.) To some extent this book constitutes an idealisation of Thomas's early years, shaded by the wistfulness of an outsider admitted for a brief while into a paradisal family world of easy-going parents and friendly children to which he can only for that period belong. Thomas himself is 'Arthur Froxfield'; but despite his heroic Christian name Arthur is essentially a visitor in the romantic Morgan world. His link with it comes through Philip Morgan, one of the seven sons—the number has a significant ring. Philip was not only Thomas's father's name and his own: it was also the name of the imaginary boy companion of his childhood, his other self. (It is interesting to compare this treatment of the theme with the more complex and romantic *Uncle Stephen* (1931) of Forrest Reid.)

The Morgan family exercise a twofold charm. On the material plane they embody a way of life cheerfully at odds with the restrictive customs of suburbia. The neighbours 'looked foul-favouredly on the house. The family was irregular, not respectable, mysterious, in short unprofitable.' The Morgans surround themselves with 'superfluous' people who 'neither produce like the poor nor consume like the rich'; theirs is a house that has no breakfast time and where a guest for an evening may stay for a month. But the Morgans are not infallible, as the odd little episode of the milk boy, recorded in Chapter Four, makes clear. In some ways this incident encapsulates the unique flavour of the book. Equally unconventional is the way in which the family are so frequently presented as one might see them in a snapshot, or through half-heard or incomplete snatches of conversation. The effect is both dream-like and curiously intimate.

Along with their unconventional challenge to materialistic social values (a challenge rather blunted for present-day readers by Thomas's failure to indicate the origin of Mr Morgan's income), the family embody the values of their Welsh background. Thomas himself came of Welsh parents, and his romantic yearning for his ancestral country became evident early on in his literary career with his wayward study, *Beautiful Wales* (1905), passages from which anticipate a good deal of the writing here. On the first page of *The Happy-Go-Lucky Morgans* we are made aware of the town of Abercorran which, by the book's end, has drawn the family back to itself; while between the Wales of Thomas's ancestry and the London of his daily toil lies Wiltshire, where he came to acquire his knowledge of, and love for, rural England. His grandparents' home is the 'Lydiard Constantine' where Arthur and Philip are most happy together; but Wiltshire also contains the New House at High Bower where the children die and the Morgans live on mysteriously as ghosts in transit.

It is against this landscape hinterland, this overlapping of imaginative worlds, that the various inset stories may most rewardingly be read. The book is in this regard very much of its time. For whereas 'The Wild Swans' is a Welsh equivalent of the Irish tales of James Stephens and W. B. Yeats, the decidedly substantial dryad whom Mr Stodham discovers in his study seems to belong to the world of E. M. Forster's early stories—but that particular Morgan's treatment of her would have been at once less enervating and more coy. Again, the book's various boyhood and garden episodes suggest the work of Kenneth Grahame and Walter de la Mare; but Edward Thomas's accounts have a dryness which theirs lack.

It is this dryness which keeps the nostalgic element from going soft. This nostalgia is bound up with the recurrent hints and suggestions as to Philip's impending death, a death that takes place at Lydiard Constantine in agricultural country half-way between the workaday London scene and the haunted landscape of Wales. The graphic nature of Thomas's account of it shows how much this country meant to him. The Welsh passages, on the other hand, have a perfervid intensity in keeping with the story of David Morgan, the eldest son of the family, who dies as a result of his attempt to discover a more elemental form of life by re-establishing contact with the ancient powers embodied in the landscape. At this point the book touches the worlds of Arthur Machen and John Cowper Powys, combining the lyrical passion of the one with the relaxed scepticism of the other. Indeed, Thomas's eloquent account of David's quest amounts to a critique of all such unbalanced romantic yearnings, a portrait of the deadly effects of a romanticism pushed too far. Not for nothing does David's tower come to be known as Morgan's Folly. So too the story of 'The Castle of Leaves' suggests a reduction of the fantasies of William Morris and Lord Dunsany to prosaic terms of logical conse-quence and wry evaluation. As a fable it is full of a not unhealthy sadness.

But in the Wiltshire passages nostalgia is more affirmatively evoked, both through the happy recollections of the boyhood scenes and, more originally, through the account towards the end of the book of Arthur's visit to the Morgans' previous home. In this episode, through a cottage woman's memories, we find them becoming sources of legend and thus mysterious and disturbing to the reader. The hitherto unknown children, Megan and Ivor, are poignant ghosts, strange and yet natural as Mrs Morgan's lamp burning in the attic window.

But it is London—Balham—which forms the true centre of the book: all the legends and memories come homing back to their source in Arthur's happy companionship with the family and in his friendship with Ann, the Welsh servant who accepts change and a new life, and who stays on after the rest of the household have returned to Abercorran. Edward Thomas is friendly to London, not only in the loving accounts of 'Our Country' and the vivid description of the long suburban road where Mr Torrance has his home, but also, still more tellingly, in his realisation that the other houses in the street where the Morgans live may have their devoted lovers also. There is nothing smug in his presentation of the Morgan family world. The fact that Ann is content to settle in London is greatly in its favour; but then Ann inhabits her own world wherever she lives. It is she who nails the book and everyone in it to a common reality. For all that, the accounts of London are more ambiguous than Ann's continuing residence might imply. If on the one hand a clump of chimney stacks can validly suggest 'a sublimer St Michael's Mount', and 'Our Country' be praised as 'supernaturally beautiful' for having 'London for a foil', so also we are made to hear the threatening roar of people and traffic that reaches up the quiet cul-de-sac where the Morgans live.

For a cul-de-sac it is: there is no way through in time or space. Seriously to wish otherwise is not Thomas's intention nor, ultimately, his desire. The London house is better than any solitary tower, and David Morgan's quest can only end in death. None the less, the book affirms by implication an eternal dimension forever apprehensible: if in 'The House of the Days of the Year' Philip himself disappears, the house does not.

It is this sense of transfigured time which unifies the book, that and the idiosyncratic, deftly glancing prose. But style alone would not prevent it from being a rag-bag; and in the end result *The Happy-Go-Lucky Morgans* is a novel which in its technique exemplifies that coincidence of mood with an understanding of the relation of time to space which informs so many novels in the modernist tradition. Casual it may seem: purposeless it is not. The imaginative world engendered by the Morgans, and with which they sustain their friends, is the book's true subject matter; and this sense of perfect integration in spite of death and failure is conveyed through the novel's subtle collocation of its various narratives. The book is less inchoate than has been supposed.

For it opens with its own conclusion, as Arthur visits Ann, now resident in the road named after the demolished Abercorran House: this novel ignores the limitations of chronology; it evokes not only past time and the years of childhood but also the enveloping spiritual and imaginative atmosphere which renders those years perennially accessible. The narrative then moves through straightforward, casual, free-associating reminiscence, broken into by the disturbing (and prophetic) story, 'The Wild Swans': a note of flight, loss, irretrievable past happiness is sounded. 'Hob-y-deri-dando' provides an interlude of youthful life and anecdote. We then return to Arthur and Ann in the abandoned house and encounter the first of the Morgans' misfit visitors, Aurelius the gipsy. (Gipsies figured much in popular literature of the time, from Theodore Watts-Dunton's best-selling *Aylwin* (1899) to the Regency romances of Jeffrey Farnol.) Next, by a natural transition, we are taken back to Ann and to the two boys' exploits in 'Our Country', many of them Thomas's own.

The technique of the book is summed up in 'Wool-Gathering', a technique of progression backwards and forwards that anticipates the work not only of Ford Madox Ford and Virginia Woolf, but also that of the Westmorland novelist, Constance Holme, whose books frequently display a sensibility akin to Thomas's own. This technique through mental association conducts us from the Morgans' library to the tranquil world of Lydiard Constantine, and so to the opposite extreme of Abercorran Town and Morgan's Folly, the elegy on vain spiritual endeavour which contains some of Thomas's most impassioned writing. But by a characteristic irony we come next to the most unsparing of Thomas's self-portraits, that of Mr Torrance; then that irony in turn is, to use Charles Williams's expression, 'defeated' by Torrance's own glowing account of village life in 'The House under the Hill', one of the best things in the book. This point of rest is followed by a counter-irony, the tale of Mr Stodham and the dryad, a story, however, with which the author seems to be ill at ease. The three fantasies which follow are examples of various genres; the formally symbolic story, the local folk tale, the romantic parable. In a brief, intense interlude that counterpoints the Welshness of the last two tales, Mr Stodham enunciates one of the book's main themes, that 'England is home and heaven too.'

There follow Philip's two tales, one of mystical vision, the other of heroic saga: here history and myth enhance each other, and in both, as elsewhere in the book, we find the pervasive image of the tower. It must be admitted, however, that this part of the novel all but founders under the weight of so much occasional narrative. But Thomas never quite loses control; he exhibits the tales as being tales merely, bringing us back to the occasion of a story's telling and to the manner of its reception. Each episode expands his portrait of the Morgan world. Then the chapter called 'What will Roland do?', with its reckoning with adult life, foreshadows the 'real' world in a manner characteristic of a number of other studies of youthful recollection; but Thomas ends his more originally than most, rounding it off with the haunted episode of Arthur's visit to High Bower, followed by a final subdued threnody at Lydiard Constantine. Philip is dead; boyhood is over; but there is no more than the ghost of a repining. Ann's final words are also the book's conclusion, in both senses of that word. There is another world, but not a better one.

> It would be blasphemous to suppose that God ever made any but the best of worlds . . . for that is impossible, say I, who have lived in Abercorran—town, house, and street—these sixty years—there is not a better world.

The Happy-Go-Lucky Morgans is a book whose charm increases with each reading. Romantic without being lush, it is pervaded by a tartness that prevents it from smacking in any way of compensatory fantasy; it accepts the facts of death and passing time for what they are, the necessary conditions of our being. (For though Mr Morgan's anger at his child's death is observed compassionately, by implication it is not endorsed.) The novel's occasional and engaging 'period' quality reminds us that these young people belong to the time of Edith Nesbit's, to mention whose name is to recall how essentially understanding and tender towards youth both writers are. No Peter Pan nostalgia haunts this book, however: 'boys forsook Abercorran House as they grew up.' But no less is there an uncontrived awareness of the mystery implicit in human experience, both among humans themselves and in relation to the inanimate world about them. The scene in which Arthur gazes out of the window of the house in Wales, while Aurelius sits reading in the library behind him, is one of the last passages of genuinely romantic prose to be written before the self-consciousness of the twentieth-century erupted.

But one does not want to discuss *The Happy-Go-Lucky Morgans* in terms of romance, even though such experiences are its matter and its theme. For this book keeps a sane grasp on regret, and can question its own emotional assumptions. It continues to be timely in the way that Thomas's poems are timely: it heralds and belongs to their achievement. Writing of himself as Mr Torrance, Thomas observes that 'His books are not the man.' This book surely is. In an age prone both to cynicism and to a sentimental clinging to the past, *The Happy-Go-Lucky Morgans* is a novel that helps one to bear and understand nostalgia. As the Wiltshire woman says of the Morgans, 'You never saw the like of them for happiness.' But she goes on to comment that, 'They did not know the sorrow and wickedness of the world as it really is.' The essence of Edward Thomas's mind and art lies in the tension between those two statements.

GLEN CAVALIERO

CHAPTER I

My story is of Balham and of a family dwelling in Balham who were more Welsh than Balhamitish. Strangers to that neighbourhood who go up Harrington Road from the tram must often wonder why the second turning on the right is called Abercorran Street: the few who know Abercorran town itself, the long grey and white street, with a castle at one end, low down by the river mouth, and an old church high up at the other, must be delighted by the memories thus recalled, but they also must wonder at the name. Abercorran Street is straight, flat, symmetrically lined on both sides by four-bedroomed houses in pairs, and it runs at right angles out of Harrington Road into another road which the pair of four-bedroomed houses visible at the corner proclaim to be exactly like it. The only external variety in the street is created by the absence from two of the cast-iron gates of any notice prohibiting the entrance of hawkers and canvassers.

When I myself first saw the white lettering on a blue ground of ABERCORRAN STREET I was perhaps more surprised than most others have been who paid any attention to it. I was surprised but not puzzled. I knew very well why it was called Abercorran Street. For I knew Abercorran House and the Morgans, its inhabitants, and the dogs and the pigeons thereof. Who that ever knew the house and the people could ever forget them? I knew the Morgans, the father and mother, the five sons, the one daughter Jessie. I knew the house down to the kitchen, because I knew old Ann, the one permanent—I had almost written immortal—servant, of whom it was said by one knowing the facts, that they also rule who only serve and wait. I knew the breakfast room where breakfast was never finished; the dark Library where they had all the magazines which have since died of their virtues; the room without a name

1

which was full of fishing-rods, walking-sticks, guns, traps, the cross-bow, boxes of skins, birds' eggs, papers, old books, pictures, pebbles from a hundred beaches, and human bones. I knew the conservatory crowded with bicycles and what had been tricycles. I knew as well as any one the pigeon-houses, the one on a pole and the one which was originally a fowl-house, built with some idea or fancy regarding profit. I knew that well-worn square of blackened gravel at the foot of the back steps, where everybody had to pass to go to the conservatory, the pigeon-houses, and the wild garden beyond, and where the sun was always shining on men and children and dogs. This square was railed off from the rest of the garden. That also I knew, its four-and-twenty elms that stood about the one oak in the long grass and buttercups and docks, like a pleasant company slowly and unwillingly preparing to leave that three-acre field which was the garden of Abercorran House and called by us The Wilderness—a name now immortalised, because the christener of streets has given it to the one beyond Abercorran Street. Under the trees lay a pond containing golden water-lilies and carp. A pond needs nothing else except boys like us to make the best of it. Yet we never could fish in it again after the strange girl was drawn out of it dead one morning: nobody knew who she was or why she had climbed over into the Wilderness to drown herself; yet Ann seemed to know, and so perhaps did the tall Roland, but both of them could lock up anything they wished to keep secret and throw away the key. I knew the elms and the one oak of the Wilderness as well as the jackdaws did. For I knew them night and day, and the birds knew nothing of them between half-past five on an October evening and half-past five the next morning.

To-day the jackdaws at least, if ever they fly that way, can probably not distinguish Abercorran Street and Wilderness Street from ordinary streets. For the trees are every one of them gone, and with them the jackdaws. The lilies and carp are no longer in the pond, and there is no pond. I can understand people cutting down trees—it is a trade and brings profit—but not draining a pond in such a garden as the Wilderness and taking all its carp home to fry in the same fat as bloaters, all for the sake of building a house that might just as well have been anywhere else or nowhere at all. I think No. 23 Wilderness Street probably has the honour and misfortune to stand in the pond's place, but they call it LYND-HURST. Ann shares my opinion, and she herself is now living in the house behind, No. 21 Abercorran Street.

Ann likes the new houses as well as the old elm-trees, and the hundreds of men, women, and children as well as the jackdaws—which is saying a good deal; for she loved both trees and birds, and I have heard her assert that the birds frequently talked in Welsh as the jackdaws used to do at the castle of Abercorran; but when I asked her why she thought so and what they said, she grew touchy and said: "Well, they did not speak English, whatever, and if it was Welsh, as I think, you cannot expect me to pervert Welsh into English, for I am no scholar." She is keeping house now for the gentleman at 21 Abercorran Street, a Mr Henry Jones. She would probably have been satisfied with him in any case, since he is the means by which Ann remains alive, free to think her own thoughts and to bake her own bread; to drink tea for breakfast, tea for dinner, tea for tea, tea for supper, and tea in between; to eat also at long intervals a quart of cockles from Abercorran shore, and a baked apple dumpling to follow; and at night to read the Welsh Bible and a Guide to the Antiquities of Abercorran. But Ann is more than satisfied because Mr Jones is Welsh. She admits his claim in spite of her unconcealed opinion that his Dolgelly Welsh, of which she can hardly understand a word, she says, is not Welsh at all. Of his speech as of the jackdaws she can retort: "He does not speak English, whatever."

Ann will never leave him unless he or she should die. She is untidy; she has never decided what is truth; and she has her own affairs as well as his to manage; but, as he says himself, he has entertained an angel unawares and she is not to be thrust out. He covers his inability to command her by asking what she could do at her age if she had to leave. It is not likely that Mr Henry Jones could get the better of a woman whom—in spite of the fact that she has never decided what is truth—he has called an angel. For he did

3

not use the word as a mere compliment, as much as to say that she was all that a woman should be when she is in domestic service. She is not; she is excellent only at pastry, which Mr Jones believes that he ought never to touch. He has been heard to call her "half angel and half bird"; but neither does this furnish the real explanation, though it offers an obvious one. For Ann is now—I mean that when we were children she seemed as old as she seems now; she limps too; and yet it might partly be her limp that made Mr Jones call her "half bird," for it is brisk and quite unashamed, almost a pretty limp; also she is pale with a shining paleness, and often she is all eyes, because her eyes are large and round and dark, looking always up at you and always a little sidelong—but that alone would not justify a sensible man in calling her "half angel." Nor would her voice, which has a remarkable unexpectedness, wherever and whenever it is heard. She begins abruptly in the middle of a thought without a word or gesture of preparation, and always on an unexpectedly high note. In this she is like the robin, who often rehearses the first half of his song in silence and then suddenly continues aloud, as if he were beginning in mid-song. Well, Mr Henry Jones, as I have said, once called her "half angel and half bird," and declared that he had entertained an angel unawares in Ann, and I believe that he is right and more than a sensible man. For he has grasped the prime fact that she is not what she seems.

For my part I can say that she is such a woman that her name, Ann Lewis, has for those who connect it with her, and with her alone, out of all the inhabitants of earth, a curious lightness, something at once pretty and old with an elfish oldness, something gay and a little weird, also a bird-like delicacy, as delicate as "linnet" and "martin." If these words are useless, remember at least that, though half bird, she is not a mere human travesty or hint of a winged thing, and that she is totally unlike any other bird, and probably unlike any other angel.

An ordinary bird certainly—and an ordinary angel probably— would have pined away at 21 Abercorran Street after having lived at Abercorran House and at Abercorran itself. But Ann is just the same as when I last saw her in Abercorran House. She alone that

4

day was unchanged. The house, the Wilderness, the conservatory, the pigeon-houses, all were changed; I was changed, but not Ann. Yet the family had then newly gone, leaving her alone in the house. It was some years since I had been there. They had been going on as ever in that idle, careless, busy life which required a big country house and an illimitable playground of moor and mountain for a full and fitting display. Gradually their friends grew up, went to a university, to business, or abroad, and acquired preferences which were not easily to be adapted to that sunny, untidy house. At first these friends would be only too glad to go round to Abercorran House of an evening after business, or a morning or two after the beginning of the vacation. Perhaps they came again, and after a long interval yet again. They said it was different: but they were wrong; it was they themselves were different; the Morgans never changed. In this way young men of the neighbourhood discovered that they were no longer boys. They could no longer put up with that careless hullabaloo of lazy, cheerful people, they took offence at the laziness, or else at the cheerfulness. Also they saw that Jessie, the girl, was as frank and untidy at seventeen as she had always been, and it took them aback, especially if they were wanting to make love to her. The thought of it made them feel foolish against their will. They fancied that she would laugh. Yet it was easy to believe that Jessie might die for love or for a lover. When somebody was pitying the girl who drowned herself in the Wilderness pond, Jessie interrupted: "She isn't a *poor girl*; she is dead; it is you are poor; she has got what she wanted, and some of you don't know what you want, and if you did you would be afraid of cold water." The young men could see the power of such words in Jessie's eye, and they did not make love to her. Some took their revenge by calling her a slut, which was what Ann used to call her when she was affectionate, as she could be to Jessie only. "Come on, there's a slut," she used to say. It was too familiar for the youths, but some of them would have liked to use it, because they felt that the phrase was somehow as amorous as it was curt, a sort of blow that was as fond as a kiss. Even when, in their hard hats at the age of twenty or so, they used the term in condemnation, they would still have given their hats for courage to speak it as Ann did, and say: "Come on, Jessie, there's a slut"; for they would have had to kiss her after the word, both because they could not help it, and for fear she should misunderstand its significance. At any rate, I believe that nobody but Ann ever addressed that term of utmost endearment to Jessie.

Thus was there one reason the less for boys who were growing up, ceasing to tear the knees of their trousers and so on, to frequent Abercorran House. I lingered on, but the death of one there had set me painfully free. After a time I used to go chiefly to honour an old custom, which proved an inadequate motive. Then year after year, of course, it was easier to put off revisiting, and one day when I went, only Ann was left. She had her kitchen and her own room; the rest of the house had no visible inhabitants. Yet Ann would not have it that it was sad. "It does a house good," she said, "to have all those Morgans in it. Now they have gone back again to Abercorran in the county of Caermarthen, and I am sure they are all happy but the mistress, and she was incurable; that was all; and there was an end of it at last." Ann herself was staying on as caretaker till Abercorran House was let or sold.

CHAPTER II

In spite of old Ann and her kitchen fire I did not stay long in the house that day. The removal which had left it deserted and silent had made it also a little sordid: the family's ways, for example, had not agreed with the wall-paper, and they had been no enemies to spiders. So I went out into the yard. There were no dogs; all had gone with the Morgans to Abercorran. The only life was a single homeless blue pigeon flying about in search of the home which had been sold. Ann said that almost every one of the birds had returned in this way, and she called the traveller into the kitchen to wait until its purchaser came in search of it. She told me who he was, and much more about the sale, which I forgot or never heard, because the sun shone very warmly into the yard just then, and I could not help seeing them all again, Jack and Roland, Lewis and Harry, and Jessie, and Philip, too, as he was at sixteen, and the dogs,—Ladas the grey-hound, Bully the bull-terrier, Granfer the dachshund, Spot the fox-terrier, and pigeons here and there among them, and some perched on roof and chimneys, some flying so high that they were no bigger than larks—and Mr Morgan at the top of the steps looking at it all and seeing that it was good. Often had I come upon them in this pattern, not knowing at first whether to join this group or that, the busy or the idle.

In those days Abercorran House stood at the end of a short, quiet street which had only six houses in it, all on the right-hand side going up, all roomy and respectable, monuments of Albert the Good's age, well covered with creepers, screened by a continuous line of limetrees and in most cases by laurel, lilac, and balsam in compact shrubberies. Opposite the houses a high wall ran along until, at Abercorran House, the street was cut short by an oak fence. Behind that fence, and occupying as much ground as all the

7

other houses and gardens together, lay the Abercorran garden, the Wilderness, which was bounded and given its triangular shape by a main road—now Harrington Road—and a farm lane. Impenetrable hedges and unscaleable fences protected the garden from the world.

I cannot say how it had come about that these three acres became attached to the house which so well deserved them. From the outside nobody would have suspected it. Abercorran House was in no practical respect superior to its neighbours; presumably the land beyond the fence was another property, or it would not have been allowed to cut short the street. But so it was. You entered the carriage gate on your right—there was no carriage—passed round the right side of the house into the yard at the back, turned to the left across it and went between the conservatory and the pigeon house out into the Wilderness.

The house was distinguished, to the casual eye, by the lack of coloured or white curtains, the never-shut gate, the flourishing, untended lilac hiding the front door and lower windows except in winter. But for me it is hard to admit that Abercorran House had anything in common, except building material, with the other five—The Elms, Orchard Lea, Brockenhurst, and Candelent Gate, and I forget the other. The street was called Candelent Street; God knows why, but there may be someone who knows as much about Candelent Gate as I do of Abercorran House.

These houses showed signs of pride and affluence. Their woodwork was frequently painted; the gravel was renewed; the knockers and letter-boxes gleamed; their inhabitants were always either neat or gaudy; even the servants were chosen half for their good looks, and were therefore continually being changed. At the Elms lived several people and a great Dane; at Orchard Lea a wire-haired terrier with a silver collar; at Candelent Gate a sort of whippet; at the house whose name I have forgotten, three pugs. These dogs all liked the Morgans' house for one reason or another: men and dogs and food were always to be found there. The dogs' owners never got so far up the street as that, though they sometimes sent to ask if Bunter the wire-haired terrier, or Lofty the Dane, or Silvermoon the whippet, were there, or to complain about one of some score of things which they disliked, as, for example, the conduct of the dogs (especially Bully, who was damned at first sight for his looks), the use of the hundred yards of roadway as a running ground, Jessie's entering the races in a costume which enabled her to win, the noise of boys whistling at the pigeons, the number of the pigeons, the visits of almost verminous-looking strangers who had forgotten the name of the house and tried The Elms, or Candelent Gate, or Orchard Lea, or Brockenhurst, before discovering the Morgans. In return, Mr Morgan regretted the nature of things and the incompatibility of temperaments, and he forbade racing in the street; but as races were always an inspiration, they recurred. As for Jessie's clothes, his opinion was that his neighbours, being fools, should look the other way or pull down their blinds. He did not see why Godiva should complain of Peeping Tom, or Peeping Tom of Godiva. As for the difficulty in remembering the name of the house, he saw no reason for changing it; all his friends and his children's friends could see instantly that neither The Elms, nor Orchard Lea, nor Brockenhurst, nor Candelent Gate, nor the other house, was his, and he could not think of consulting those who were not his friends.

Abercorran House was honoured by four martins' nests under the eaves, placed at such regular intervals that they appeared to be corbels for supporting the roof. Not one of the other houses in the street had a martin's nest. But the distinguishing feature of the Morgans' house was that you could see at a glance that it was the Morgans'. The front garden was merely a way round to the yard and the Wilderness. Altogether the front of the house, facing east, must have looked to a stranger uninhabited. Everything was done on the other side, or in the yard. Bounded on the east by the house, on the north or Brockenhurst side by a high wall (built by Mr Brockenhurst, as we called him), and on the west or lane side by a split oak fence, but separated from the Wilderness and the south only by the conservatory and the pigeon-house and some low railings, the yard of Abercorran House was a reservoir of sun. The high south wall was occupied, not by fruit trees, but by cascades of ivy and by men and boys standing or sitting in the sun, talking, watching the jackdaws coming and going in the elms of the Wilderness, and also by dogs gnawing bones or sleeping. There was no cultivated garden, but several of the corners had always some blossoms of wall-flower, sweet-rocket, or snapdragon, that looked after themselves: in the pocket between the fence and the pigeon house half a dozen sunflowers invariably found a way of growing eight feet high and expanding enormous blossoms, every one of them fit to be copied and stuck up for a sign outside the "Sun" inn.

Nobody could mistake Abercorran House; but in case anybody did, Mr Morgan had a brass plate with "T. Ll. Morgan" on it at the foot of his front steps, in a position where to see it from the road was impossible. This plate was always bright: the only time when I saw it dim was when Ann was alone in the deserted house. A succession of active, dirty, little maids employed in the house agreed upon this one point, that the name-plate must be polished until it reflected their cheeks as they reflected its never-understood glory. No vainglorious initial letters followed the name, nor any descriptive word. The maids—Lizz, Kate, Ellen, Polly, Hannah, Victoria, and the rest—probably knew no more than I ever did why the name was there. For it was perfectly clear that Mr Morgan never did or wished to do anything. The name might just as well have been that of some famous man born there a hundred years before: in any case it had nothing to do with that expression the house had of frankness, mystery, untidiness, ease, and something like rusticity. In the yard behind, the bull terrier stood for frankness, the greyhound for rusticity, the cats for mystery, and most things for untidiness, and all for ease.

Indoors it was a dark house. Windows were numerous, but it was undoubtedly dark. This was in part due to comparison with the outer air, where people lived as much as possible, and especially with the sunlit yard. The house had, however, a dark spirit, aided by the folds of heavy curtains, the massive, old, blackened furniture, and the wall-paper of some years before. You wandered as you pleased about it, alone or with Philip, Lewis, or Harry. Most of the rooms were bedrooms, but not conspicuous as such when strewn with cases of butterflies, birds' eggs and nests, stuffed animals, cages containing foreign birds, several blackbirds, a nest of young thrushes, an adder and some ringed snakes and lizards, a hedgehog, white and piebald rats and mice, fishing-rods and tackle, pistols and guns and toy cannon, tools and half-made articles of many kinds, model steam-engines, a model of the "Victory" and a painting of the "Owen Glendower" under a flock of sail, boxing gloves, foils, odds and ends of wood and metal, curiosities from tree and stone, everything that can be accumulated by curious and unruly minds; and then also the owners themselves and their friends, plotting, arguing, examining their property, tending the living animals or skinning the dead, boxing, fencing, firing cannon, and going to and fro.

The kitchen, the Library, and Mrs Morgan's room were silent rooms. In the kitchen Ann ruled. It smelt of an old Bible and new cakes: its sole sound was Ann's voice singing in Welsh, which was often stopped abruptly by her duties coming to a head, or by something outside—as when she heard Lewis overtaxing Granfer in teaching it a trick and flitted out, saying: "Don't use the dog like that. Anyone might think he had no human feelings." She must have been, in a sense, young in those days, but was unlike any other young woman I have seen, and it never occurred to me then to think of her as one; nor, as certainly, did it seem possible that she would grow old—and she has not grown old. When she left her kitchen it was seldom to go out. Except to do the household shopping, and that was always after dark, she never went beyond the yard. She did not like being laughed at for her looks and accent, and she disliked London so much as to keep out the London air, as far as possible, with closed windows.

I do not remember ever to have seen Ann talking to her mistress, and no doubt she did without her. Mrs Morgan was not to be seen about the house, and her room was perfectly respected. She sat at the window looking on to the yard and watched the boys as she sewed, or read, or pretended to read. Sometimes Jessie sat with her, and then I have seen her smiling. She had large eyes of a gloomy lustre which looked as if they had worn their hollows in the gaunt

11

face by much gazing and still more musing. The boys were silent for a moment as they went past her door. I do not know when she went out, if she ever did, but I never saw her even in the yard. Nor did I see her with Mr Morgan, and it was known that he was never in her sitting-room. She seemed to live uncomplaining under a weight of gloom, looking out from under it upon her strong sons and their busy indolence, with admiration and also a certain dread.

Jessie was the favourite child of father and mother, but I used to think that it was to avoid her father that she was so often in her mother's room. Why else should such a child of light and liberty stay in that quietness and dark silence which breathed out darkness over the house? Outside that room she was her brothers' equal in boldness, merriment and even in strength. Yet it once struck me with some horror, as she sat up at the window, that she was like her mother—too much like her—the dark eyes large, the cheeks not any too plump, the expression sobered either by some fear of her own or by the conversation; it struck me that she might some day by unimaginable steps reach that aspect of soft endurance and tranquilly expectant fear. At fifteen, when I best remember her, she was a tall girl with a very grave face when alone, which could break out with astonishing ease into great smiles of greeting and then laughter of the whole soul and body as she was lured to one group or another in the yard. She mixed so roughly and carelessly with every one that, at first, I, who had false picture-book notions of beauty and looked for it to have something proud and ceremonious in itself and its reception, did not see how beautiful she was. She took no care of her dress, and this made all the more noticeable the radiant sweetness of her complexion. But I recognised her beauty before long. One Saturday night she was shopping with Ann, and I met her suddenly face to face amidst a pale crowd all spattered with acute light and shadow from the shops. I did not know who it was, though I knew Ann. She was so extraordinary that I stared hard at her as people do at a foreigner, or a picture, or an animal, not expecting a look in answer. Others also were staring, some of the women were laughing. There could be no greater testimony to beauty than this laughter of the vulgar. The vulgar always laugh at beauty; that they did so is my only reason for calling these women by that hateful name. Jessie did not heed them. Then she caught sight of me, and her face lightened and blossomed with smiles. I shall not forget it, and how I blushed to be so saluted in that vile street. There was another reason why I should remember. Some of the big boys and young men—boys just leaving the Grammar School or in their first year at an office— winked at her as they passed; and one of them, a white-faced youth with a cigarette, not only winked but grinned as if he were certain of conquest. Jessie's face recovered its grave look, she gave Ann her basket, and at the fullness of his leer she struck him in the mouth with all her force, splashing her small hand and his face with blood. I trembled and winced with admiration. Jessie burst into tears. The crowd was quiet and excited. Everybody seemed to be looking for somebody else to do they could not tell what. The crush increased. I saw Ann wiping Jessie's hand. They were saved by a big red-faced working woman, who had a little husband alongside of her. She pushed very slowly but with great determination through the crowd, using her husband rather as an addition to her weight than as a brother in arms, until she came to the cluster of moody youths. Between us and them she stood, and hammering in her words with a projecting chin, told them to "Get home, you chalk-faced quill-drivers, and tell your mothers to suckle you again on milk instead of water. Then you can ask leave to look at girls, but not the likes of this beautiful dear, not you. Get home. . . ." They laughed awkwardly and with affected scorn as they turned away from that face on fire; and it was laughing thus that they realised that they were blocking the traffic, and therefore dispersed muttering a sort of threats, the woman keeping up her attack until it could not be hoped that they heard her. As we hurried home we were hooted by similar boys and by some of the young women who matched them.

We were proud of Jessie in this attitude, which made her father call her "Brynhild" or "Boadicea." When she was with her mother she was "Cordelia:" when she nursed a cat or fed the pigeons she was "Phyllis," by which I suppose he meant to express her

13

gentleness. From that Saturday night I admired everything about her, down to her bright teeth, which were a little uneven, and thus gave a touch of country homeliness to her beauty. Very few girls came to Abercorran House to see Jessie, partly because she was impatient of very girlish girls, partly because they could not get on with her brothers. And so, with all her sweet temper—and violence that came like a tenth wave—she was rather alone; just as her face dropped back to gravity so completely after laughter, so I think she returned to solitude very easily after her romps. Was it the shadow of London upon her, or of her mother's room? She went back to Wales too seldom, and as for other holidays, the charming sophisticated home-counties were nothing to the Morgans, nor the seaside resorts. Jessie should have had a purer air, where perhaps she would never have sung the song beginning, "O the cuckoo, she's a pretty bird," and ending with the chorus:

"Oh, the cuckoo, she's a pretty bird, she singeth as she flies:
She bringeth good tidings, she telleth no lies."

Sometimes she was willing to sing all three verses and repeat the first to make a fourth and to please herself:

"Oh, the cuckoo, she's a pretty bird, she singeth as she flies:
She bringeth good tidings, she telleth no lies:
She sucketh sweet flowers, for to keep her voice clear;
And the more she singeth cuckoo, the summer draweth
    near."

When she came to those last two lines I looked at her very hard, inspired by the thought that it was she had sucked dew out of the white flowers of April, the cuckoo-flower, the stitchwort, the blackthorn, and the first may, to make her voice clear and her lips sweet. While she sang it once Mr Stodham—a clerk somewhere who had seen a naked Dryad—bent his head a little to one side, perfectly motionless, the eyes and lips puckered to a perfect attention, at once eager and passive, so that I think the melody ran

14

through all his nerves and his veins, as I am sure he was inviting it to do. I heard him telling Mr Morgan afterwards that he wanted to cry, but could not, it was not in his family.

That was in Mr Morgan's own room, the library, the largest room in the house, where Mr Stodham had gone to escape the boys for a time. When Mr Morgan was not at the top of the steps which led down to the yard, smoking a cigar and watching the boys, the dogs, and the pigeons, and looking round now and then to see if Jessie would come, he was in the library sitting by the big fire with a cigar and a book. If anyone entered he put the book on his knee, shifted the cigar to the middle of his mouth, removed his spectacles, and looked at us without a word. Then with a nod he replaced book, cigar, and spectacles, and ignored us. We spoke in whispers or not at all as we coasted the high book-shelves lining every part of each wall, except in one corner, where there were several guns, an ivory-handled whip, and a pair of skates. The books were on the whole grim and senatorial. We felt them vaguely—the legal, the historical, and the classical tiers—to be our accusers and judges. There were also many sporting books, many novels, plays, poems, and romances of

"Old loves and wars for ladies done by many a lord."

If we took some of these down they were not to be read in the library. We laid one on our knees, opened a page, but glanced up more than once the while at Mr Morgan, and then either replaced it or put it under an arm and ran off with it on tiptoe. "Stay if you like, boys," said Mr Morgan as we reached the door; and immediately after, "Shut the door quietly. Good-bye."

At most gatherings and conversations Mr Morgan listened in silence, except when appealed to for a fact or a decision, or when he laughed—we often did not know why—and dropped his cigar, but caught it in some confusion at his waist. He was a lean man of moderate height and very upright, a hawk's profile, a pointed brown beard, cheeks weathered and worn, and the heaviest-lidded eyes possible without deformity. He stood about with one hand in

15

his coat pocket, the other holding a newspaper or an opened book. The dogs loved him and leaped up at him when he appeared, though he took small notice of them. When we met him in the street he always had a slow horseman's stride, was wrapped in a long overcoat and deep in thought, and never saw us or made any sign. At home, though he was a severe-looking man of grave speech, he accepted the irregularities and alarums without a murmur, often with a smile, sometimes, as I have said, with laughter, but that was a little disconcerting. It was on questions of sport and natural history that he was most often asked for a judgment, which he always gave with an indifferent air and voice, yet in a very exact and unquestionable manner. But they were the frankest family alive, and there was nothing which the elder boys would not discuss in his presence or refer to him—except in the matter of horse-racing. Jack and Roland, the two eldest sons, betted; and so, as we all knew, did Mr Morgan; but the father would not say one word about a horse or a race, unless it was a classical or curious one belonging to the past.

CHAPTER III

One day as I was passing the library door with a pair of swan's wings belonging to Philip, Mr Morgan stepped out. The look which he gave to the wings and to me compelled me to stop, and he said:

"You have a pair of wild swans there, Arthur."

I said I had.

"Swan's wings," he repeated. "Swan's wings;" and as he uttered the words his body relaxed more than ordinary, until the middle of his back was supported against the wall, his feet and face stuck out towards me.

"Did you know," said he, "that some women had swan's wings with which to fly?"

Now I had heard of swan maidens, but he distinctly said "women," and the tone of his voice made me feel that he was not referring to the flimsy, incredible creatures of fairy tales, but to women of flesh and blood, of human stature and nature, such women as might come into the library and stand by Mr Morgan's fire—only, so far as I knew, no women ever did. So I said "No."

"They have," said he, "or they had in the young days of Elias Griffiths, who was an old man when I was a lad."

Here he sighed and paused, but apologised, though not exactly to me, by saying: "But that"—meaning, I suppose, the sigh—"is neither here nor there. Besides, I must not trespass in Mr Stodham's province." For Mr Stodham was then passing, and I made way for him.

Mr Morgan continued:

"It was on a Thursday. . . ."

Now I held Mr Morgan in great respect, but the mention of Thursday at the opening of a story about swan maidens was too much for me.

"Why Thursday?" I asked.

"I agree with the boy," remarked Mr Stodham, leaving us and the talk of swan maidens and Thursday.

Thursday was a poor sort of a day. Saturday, Sunday, Monday, were all noticeable days in some way, though not equally likeable. Friday, too, as, ushering in Saturday and the end of the week, had some merit. Wednesday, again, was a half holiday. But least of all was to be said for Thursday. Mr Morgan's answer was:

"I said it was on a Thursday, because it was on a Thursday and not on any other day. I am sorry to see that the indolent spirit of criticism has resorted to you. Pluck it out, my boy. . . . Give me those wings . . . They are beautiful: I expect the ferryman shot the swans in the estuary at Abercorran. . . . However, they are not large enough. . . ."

He was looking carefully at the wings, thinking things which he could not say to me, and I said nothing. Then, handing me back the wings, he went on:

"It was on a Thursday, a very stormy one in December, that two young men who lived with their old mothers a mile or two inland went down to the rocks to shoot with their long, ancient guns. They shot some trash. But the wind for the most part snatched the birds from the shot or the shot from the birds, and they could not hold their guns still for cold. They continued however, to walk in and out among the rocks, looking for something to prevent them saving their gunpowder. But they saw nothing more until they were close to a creek that runs up into the cliff and stops you unless you have wings. So there they stopped and would have turned back, if one of them had not gone to the very edge of the creek wall and looked down. He levelled his gun instantly, and then dropped it again. His companion coming up did the same. Two white swans—not gray ones like this—were just alighting upon the sand below, and before the eyes of the young men they proceeded to lay aside their wings and entered the water, not as swans, but as women, upon that stormy Thursday. They were women with long black hair, beautiful white faces and—Have you seen the statues at the Museum, my boy? Yes, you have; and you never thought that

18

there was anything like them outside of marble. But there is. These women were like them, and they were not of marble, any more than they were of what I am made of." His own skin was coloured apparently by a mixture of weather and cigar smoke. "These women were white, like the moon when it is neither green nor white. Now those young men were poor and rough, and they were unmarried. They watched the women swimming and diving and floating as if they had been born in the sea. But as it began to darken and the swimmers showed no signs of tiring, the young men made their way down to the swans' wings to carry them off. No sooner had they picked up the wings than the two women hastened towards them into the shallow water, crying out something in their own tongue which the men could not even hear for the roar of winds and waters. As the women drew nearer, the men retreated a little, holding the wings behind them, but keeping their eyes fixed on the women. When the women actually left the water the men turned and made for home, followed by the owners of the wings. They reached their cottages in darkness, barred the doors, and put away the wings.

But the wingless ones knocked at the doors, and cried out until the old mothers heard them. Then the sons told their tale. Their mothers were very wise. Fumbling to the bottom of their chests they found clothes suitable for young women and brides, and they opened their doors. They quieted the women with clothes for wings, and though they were very old they could see that the creatures were beautiful as their sons had said. They took care that the wings were not discovered.

Those young men married their guests, and the pairs lived happily. The sons were proud of their wives, who were as obedient as they were beautiful. Said the old women: Anybody might think they still had their wings by their lightsome way of walking. They made no attempt to get away from the cottages and the smell of bacon. In fact, they were laughed at by the neighbours for their home-keeping ways; they never cared to stay long or far from home, or to see much of the other women. When they began to have children they were worse than ever, hardly ever leaving the house and never parting from their children. They got thin as well as pale; a stranger could hardly have told that they were not human, except for the cold, greenish light about them and their gait which was like the swimming of swans.

In course of time the old women died, having warned their sons not to let their wives on any account have the wings back. The swan-women grew paler and yet more thin. One of them, evidently in a decline, had at length to take to her bed. Here for the first time she spoke of her wings. She begged to be allowed to have them back, because wearing them, she said, she would certainly not die. She cried bitterly for the wings, but in vain. On her deathbed she still cried for them, and took no notice of the minister's conversation, so that he, in the hope of gaining peace and a hearing, advised her husband to give way to her. He consented. The wings were taken out of the chest where they had been exchanged for a wedding garment years before; they were as white and unruffled as when they lay upon the sand. At the sight of them the sick woman stood up in her bed with a small, wild cry. The wings seemed to fill the room with white waves; they swept the rushlight away as they carried the swan out into the wind. All the village heard her flying low above the roofs towards the sea, where a fisherman saw her already high above the cliffs. It was the last time she was seen.

The other swan-wife lingered for a year or two. A sister of her husband's kept house in her place. Whether this woman had not heard the story or did not believe it, I do not know. One day, however, she discovered the wings and gave them to the children to play with. As one child came in soon afterwards crying for his mother and the wings at the same time, it was certain that she also had taken flight to some place more suitable for wild swans. They say that two generations of children of these families were famous for the same beautiful walking as their mothers, whom they never saw again. . . ." Here Mr Morgan paused for a moment then added: "I wonder why we never hear of swan-men?"

I was not much impressed at the time by the story and his dry way of telling it. What I liked most was the idea that two ordinary men went shooting on a Thursday in mid-winter and caught swan-maidens bathing in a pool on the Welsh coast and married them. So I said to Mr Morgan:

"Why did you ever leave Wales, Mr Morgan?"

He put a new cigar severely between his teeth and looked at me as if he did not know or even see me. I ran off with the wings to Philip.

CHAPTER IV

HOB-Y-DERI-DANDO[1]

I ALONE was listening to the swan story, but it would have been more in accordance with the custom of the house if it had been told in a large company out in the yard—in one of the bedrooms—in the library itself—or in the dining-room (where there was a vast sideboard bearing a joint, cheese, bread, fruit, cakes, and bottles of ale, to which the boys or the visitors resorted, for meals without a name, at all hours of the day). Most often the yard and the steps leading down to it were the meeting-place. The pigeons, the conservatory, with its bicycles, a lathe and all sorts of beginnings and remains, the dogs, above all the sun and the view of the Wilderness, attracted everyone to the yard as a common centre for the Morgans and those who gathered round one or other of them. Thus, for example, the pigeons did not belong to the Morgans at all, but to one Higgs, who was unable to keep them at his home. He was always in and out of the yard, frequently bringing friends who might or might not become friends of the family. Everyone was free to look at the pigeons, note which had laid and which had hatched, to use the lathe, to take the dogs out if they were willing, to go upstairs and see the wonders—the eggs of kites, ravens, buzzards, curlews, for example, taken by Jack and Roland near Abercorran—and to have a meal at the sideboard or a cup of tea from one of Ann's brews in the kitchen.

Jack and Roland in themselves attracted a large and mixed company. Jack, the eldest, was a huge, brown-haired, good-natured fellow, with his father's eyes, or rather eyelids. He was very strong, and knew all about dogs and horses. He was a good deal away from the house, we did not know where, except that it was

[1] i.e. *Hey-derry-down*, or *Upsa-daisy-dando*.

22

not at an office or other place where they work. Roland was tall, black-haired, dark-eyed like his mother, and as strong as Jack. He was handsome and proud-looking, but though quick-tempered was not proud in speech with us lesser ones. His learning was equal to Jack's, and it comprised also the theatre; he was dressed as carefully as Jack was carelessly, but like Jack would allow the pigeons to perch anywhere upon him. Both wore knickerbockers and looked like country gentlemen in exile. Jack smoked a clay pipe, Roland cigarettes. They were very good friends. Though they did no work, one or other of them was often at the lathe. They boxed together while we stood round, admiring Jack because he could never be beaten, and Roland because no one but his brother could have resisted him. They were sometimes to be seen looking extremely serious over a sporting paper. Lewis and Harry were a similar pair many years younger, Lewis, the elder, broader, shorter, and fairer of the two, both of them stiff and straight like their elders. They also had begun to acquire trains of adherents from the various schools which they had irregularly and with long intervals attended. They treated the streets like woods, and never complained of the substitute. Once or twice a year they went to a barber to have their black and brown manes transformed into a uniform stubble of less than half an inch. Midway between these two pairs came Philip, and a little after him Jessie.

These six attracted every energetic or discontented boy in the neighbourhood. Abercorran House was as good as a mountain or a sea-shore for them, and was accessible at any hour of the day or night, "except at breakfast time," said Mr Stodham—for there was no breakfast-time. Mr Stodham was a middle-aged refugee at Abercorran House, one for whom breakfast had become the most austere meal of the day, to be taken with a perfectly adjusted system of times and ceremonies, in silence, far from children and from all innovation, irregularity, and disorder. Therefore the house of the Morgans was for him the house that had no breakfast-time, and unconsciously he was seeking salvation in the anarchy which at home would have been unendurable. Mr Stodham was not the only client who was no longer a boy, but he and the few others were

all late converts; for, as I have mentioned, boys forsook Abercorran House as they grew up. Parents, too, looked foul-favouredly on
the house. The family was irregular, not respectable, mysterious,
in short unprofitable. It may have got about that when Mr Morgan
once received a fountain-pen as a gift, he said he did not want any
of "your damned time-saving appliances." Of course, said he, some
people could not help saving time and money—let them—they
were never clever enough to know what to do with them, supposing that their savings were not hidden out of their reach like their
childhood—but it had not occurred to him to do either, so he gave
the pen to the little milk-boy, advising him to give it away before it
got a hold on him. This child had delighted Mr Morgan by coming
up the street every day, singing a filthy song. It was a test of
innocence, whether the words of it did or did not make the hearer
wish that either he or the singer might sink instantaneously into
the earth. Mr Morgan did not like the song at all. The words were
in no way better than those of a bad hymn, nor was the tune. But
he liked what he called the boy's innocence. Ophelia only sang "By
Gis and by Saint Charity" under cover of madness. At the worst
this boy made no pretence. Mr Morgan argued, probably, that one
who had such thoughts would not have the impudence to sing so
except to a select audience; he had no doubt of this when the boy
sang it once on being asked to in the Library. I do not know what
happened, beyond this, that Mr Morgan looked as if he had been
crying, and the boy never sang it again. If this got about, few could
think any better of the Morgans at Abercorran House. Moreover,
the window frames and doors were never painted, and the front
gate remained upright only because it was never closed; and on any
sunny day a man passing down the lane was sure of hearing men
and boys laughing, or Jessie singing, and dogs barking or yawning,
pigeons courting, over the fence.

CHAPTER V

WE recalled many memories. Ann and I, as we stood in the empty and silent, but still sunlit yard, on my last visit. At one moment the past seemed everything, the present a dream; at another, the past seemed to have gone for ever. Trying, I suppose, to make myself believe that there had been no break, but only a gradual change, I asked Ann if things at Abercorran House had not been quieter for some time past.

"Oh no," said she, "there was always someone new dropping in, and you know nobody came twice without coming a hundred times. We had the little Morgans of Clare's Castle here for more than a year, and almost crowded us out with friends. Then Mr—whatever was his name—the Italian—I mean the Gypsy—Mr Aurelius—stayed here three times for months on end, and that brought quite little children."

"Of course it did, Ann. Aurelius . . . Don't I remember what he was—can it be fifteen years ago? He was the first man I ever met who really proved that man is above the other animals *as an animal*. He was really better than any pony, or hound, or bird of prey, in their own way."

"Now you are *talking*, Mr Froxfield—Arthur, I *should* say."

"I suppose I am, but Aurelius makes you talk. I remember him up in the Library reading that Arabian tale about the great king who had a hundred thousand kings under him, and what he liked most was to read in old books about Paradise and its wonders and loveliness. I remember Aurelius saying: And when he came upon a certain description of Paradise, its pavilions and lofty chambers and precious-laden trees, and a thousand beautiful and strange things, he fell into a rapture so that he determined to make its equal on earth."

25

"He is the first rich man I ever heard of that had so much sense," said Ann. "Perhaps Aurelius would have done like that if he had been as rich as sin, instead of owing a wine-and-spirit merchant four and six and being owed half-a-crown by me. But he does not need it now, that is, so far as we can tell."

"What, Ann, is Aurelius dead?"

"That I cannot say. But we shall never see him again."

"Why frighten me for nothing? Of course he will turn up: he always did."

"That is impossible."

"Why?"

"He promised Mr Torrance he would write and wait for an answer every Midsummer day, if not oftener, wherever he might be. He has now missed two Midsummers, which he would not do—you know he could not do such a thing to Mr Torrance—if he was in his right mind. He wasn't young, and perhaps he had to pay for keeping his young looks so long."

"Why? How old could he be?" I said quickly, forgetting how long ago it was that I met him first.

"I know he is fifty," said Ann.

I did not answer because it seemed ridiculous and I did not want to be rude to Ann. I should have said a moment before, had I been asked, that he was thirty. But Ann was right.

"Where was he last heard of, Ann?"

"I went myself with little Henry Morgan and Jessie to a place called Oatham, or something like it, where he last wrote from. He had been an under-gardener there for nearly two years, and we saw the man and his wife who let him a room and looked after him. They said he seemed to be well-off, and of course he would. You know he ate little, smoked and drank nothing, and gave nothing to any known charities. They remembered him very well because he taught them to play cards and was very clean and very silent. "As clean as a lady," she said to Jessie, who only said, "Cleaner.' You know her way. The man did not like him, I know. He said Aurelius used to sit as quiet as a book and never complained of anything. 'He never ate half he paid for, I will say that,' said he. 'He was too fond

26

of flowers, too, for an under-gardener, and used to ask why daisies and fluellen and such-like were called weeds. There was something wrong with him, something on his conscience perhaps.' The squire's agent, a Mr Theobald, said the same when he came in. He thought there was something wrong. He said such people were unnecessary. Nothing could be done with them. They were no better than wild birds compared with pheasants, even when they could sing, which some of them could do, but not Aurelius. They caused a great deal of trouble, said my lord the agent of my lord the squire, yet you couldn't put them out of the way. He remarked that Aurelius never wrote any letters and never received any—that looked bad, too. 'What we want,' said he—'is a little less Theobald,' said Jessie, but the man didn't notice her. 'What we want is efficiency. How are we to get it with the likes of this Mr What's-his-name in the way? They neither produce like the poor nor consume like the rich, and it is by production and consumption that the world goes round, I say. He was a bit of a poacher, too. I caught him myself letting a hare out of a snare—letting it out, so he said. I said nothing to the squire, but the chap had to go.' And that's all we shall hear about Aurelius," said Ann. "He left there in the muck of February. They didn't know where he was going, and didn't care, though he provided them with gossip for a year to come. The woman asked me how old he was. Before I could have answered, her husband said: 'About thirty I should say.' The woman could not resist saying snappily: 'Fifty' . . ."

Aurelius was gone, then. It cannot have surprised anyone. What was surprising was the way he used to reappear after long absences. While he was present everyone liked him, but he had something unreal about him or not like a man of this world. When that squire's agent called his under-gardener a superfluous man, he was a brute and he was wrong, but he saw straight. If we accept his label there must always have been some superfluous men since the beginning, men whom the extravagant ingenuity of creation has produced out of sheer delight in variety, by-products of its immense processes. Sometimes I think it was some of these superfluous men who invented God and all the gods and godlets. Some of them have been killed, some enthroned, some sainted, for it. But in a civilisation like ours the superfluous abound and even flourish. They are born in palace and cottage and under hedges. Often they are fortunate in being called mad from early years; sometimes they live a brief, charmed life without toil, envied almost as much as the animals by drudges; sometimes they are no more than delicate instruments on which men play melodies of agony and sweetness.

The superfluous are those who cannot find society with which they are in some sort of harmony. The magic circle drawn round us all at birth surrounds these in such a way that it will never overlap, far less become concentric with, the circles of any other in the whirling multitudes. The circle is a high wall guarded as if it were a Paradise, not a Hell, "with dreadful faces thronged and fiery arms": or it is no more than a shell border round the garden of a child, and there is no one so feeble but he can slip over it, or shift it, or trample it down, though powerless to remove it. Some of these weaker ones might seem to have several circles enclosing them, which are thus upset or trampled one by one as childhood advances. Everybody discovers that he can cross their borders. They do not retaliate. These are the superfluous who are kept alive to perform the most terrible or most loathsome tasks. Rarely do their tyrants see their eyes gleaming in their dungeons, and draw back or hurl a stone like a man who has almost trodden upon a fox.

But the superfluous are not always unfortunate; we who knew Aurelius would never call him unfortunate. There are some—and more than ever in these days when even the strongest do not condemn outright, and when deaths less unpleasant to the executioner have been discovered—some who escape the necessity to toil and spin for others, and do not spend their ease in manacles. Many of the women among the hunted are not slaughtered as soon as caught. They are kept in artfully constructed and choicely decorated cages where their captors try to force them to sing over and over again the notes which were their allurement at first; a few survive to wear white locks and trouble with a new note the serenity of the palaces where their cages are suspended. The superfluous have been known to learn the ways of their superiors, to make little camps unmolested in the midst of the foreign land, to enjoy a life admired of many and sometimes envied, but insincerely.

Some of the captives enslave their masters. Aurelius was one. From my earliest days Aurelius and rumours of him were much about me. Once he earned his bread in a great country house by looking after the books and writing letters. They lodged, fed, and clothed him, and gave him a small wage—he came from no one knew where, except that it must have been a gutter or a ditch, as he said, "between the moon and Mercury." But he would tell children that he was begotten out of the moonlight by an owl's hooting, or that he was born in a tent in the New Forest, where there were more leaves than money. It was a sort of grievance against him that he could always buy what he wanted, as a book for himself or a toy for a child.

He can have been of little use as a letter-writer, as I see now. His writing looked as unfamiliar as Persian, and must have been laborious. It was suited to the copying of incantations, horoscopes, receipts for confectionery. It must often have startled the reader like a line of trees or flight of birds writing their black legend on the dawn silver. There was nothing in the meaning of his sentences, I think, to correspond with the looks of them. A few of his letters survive, and some notes on accessions to the library, etc.; but it is clear that they were written in a language foreign to the man, a loose journalistic English of the moment, neither classic nor colloquial, and they have no significance.

Some people called him a little man, but in his size as in other things he seemed rather to be of another species than a diminutive example of our own. He was smaller than a man, but not unpleasantly small, neither were his hands too long and delicate, nor were they incapable of a man's work. In every way he was finely made and graceful, with clear large features, curled dark-brown hair and beard almost auburn. His clothes were part of him, of a lighter brown than his hair and of some substance which was more like a natural fur than a made cloth. These clothes, along with his voice, which was very deep, his hair, and his silent movements, increased his pleasing inhumanity. He sat among many people and said trivial things, or more often nothing, looking very far away and very little, turning all light somehow to moonlight, his dark eyes full of subdued gleaming; and both speech and silence drew upon him an attention which gave the casual observer an excuse for calling him vain. Children liked him, though he never troubled to show a liking for children, and while we sat on his lap or displayed a book for him he would be talking busily to others, but without offending us. He did not often tell us tales or play games with us, but he had a swift, gentle way of putting his hand on our heads and looking at us which always seemed an honour.

I recall chiefly, in connection with Aurelius, an evening near the end of winter at the great house. There had been a week of frost, some days silent and misty, others loud and clear with a north-east wind. Then came the west wind, a day's balmy sun, and at last rain. This day I recall was the next. It was full of goings to and fro of loose cloud, of yellow threatenings on the hills. The light was thin and pale, falling tenderly over green fields and their fresh sprinkling of mole-heaps. But the rain would not descend, and as we got to the big house for tea the sky cleared, and in the twilight blackbirds were chinking nervously before sleep and now and then hurrying across the dim grass between the dark hedges and copses. A robin sang at the edge of a holly, and a thrush somewhere remote, and the world had become narrow and homely, the birds sounded secure like happily tired boys lazily undressing, and evidently they did not expect men. Three-quarters of a moon hung at the zenith, cold and fresh and white like an early spring flower. We grew silent, but at tea were particularly noisy and excited, too excited and near to tears, when I rushed upstairs. In the library I found Aurelius reading, with his back to the uncurtained window, by a light that only illuminated his face and page. Running at first to the window, I pressed my face on the pane to see the profound of deepening night, and the lake shining dimly like a window through which the things under the earth might be seen if you were out. The abyss of solitude below and around was swallowing the little white moon and might swallow me also; with terror at this feeling I turned away. "What?" said Aurelius, without even looking round, but apparently aware of my feeling. Seated in his lap, he took hardly more notice of me, but I was comforted. His silence was not a mere absence of words. It was not the peevish silence of one too cautious or too fearful to speak; nor the silence of one who has suddenly become isolated and feels it, yet cannot escape. Up out of the silence rose the voice of Aurelius reading out of the book before him. Over my shoulder came the rustling of ivy, and the sighing of trees, and the running of the brook through the coomb; the moon, close at hand, out in the black garden, pressed her face against the window and looked in at me. Aurelius was reading of that great king who had under him a hundred thousand kings, and whose chief delight was in ancient books telling of the loveliness of Paradise: "And when he met with this description of the world to come, and of Paradise and its pavilions, its lofty chambers, its trees and fruits, and of the other things in Paradise, his heart enticed him to construct its like on earth . . ." The world extended to a vastness that came close up to me and enfolded me as a lake enfolds one swan. Thus at the building of that Paradise I easily imagined doorways that would have admitted Orion and the Pleiades together. And at last, at the cry of destruction, though I was sorry, I was intensely satisfied with both the sadness and the splendour. I began to dream in the following silence. I dreamed I was lying at the edge of an immense sea, upon a rock scarcely raised above the water of the colour of sapphires. I saw go by me a procession of enormous seals whose backs swelled out of the wavelets like camels, and as they passed in deep water, a few yards away, each one cast on me his dark soft eyes, and they were the eyes of Aurelius. There were more coming behind when I awoke. Aurelius lighted another lamp. I went over again to the window and looked out. In a flash I saw the outer vast world of solitude, darkness, and silence, waiting eternally for its prey, and felt behind me the little world within that darkness like a lighthouse. I went back to the others. Aurelius for all I knew went to the kingdoms of the moon.

Many times again he read to us after I had on some pretext brought him to Abercorran House, a year or two later.

Yet older people said that Aurelius had no perception of religion, or beauty, or human suffering. Certainly he talked of these things, as I see now, with a strange and callous-seeming familiarity, as a poultry-farmer talks of chickens; but our elders did not explain it when they called it in scorn artistic. I suspect it was in scorn, though they said it was to humanise him, that they helped to get him married to a "nice sensible" girl who never came near Abercorran House. Like many other women, she had been used to petting him as if he were an animal. He responded with quaint, elaborate speeches and gestures, kneeling to speak, calling her by different invented names, but perhaps with a mock-heroic humorous gleam. He married her, and all I know is that he slipped away from the charming flat where the kindness of friends had deposited them, and never reappeared in the neighbourhood except at Abercorran House. He sent her money from time to time which he earned as trainer to a troupe of dogs in a travelling circus, as a waiter, as a commercial traveller of some sort. It was said that he had been to sea. In any case, to hear him sing

"Along the plains of Mexico"

was better than sailing in any ship we had ever been in or imagined. I am sure that he could not have improved his singing of "Along the Plains of Mexico" by sailing from Swansea to Ilfracombe or round Cape Horn, or by getting a heart of oak and a hand of iron. He brought nothing back with him from his travels. He had no possessions—not a book, not a watch, not an extra suit of clothes, not a lead pencil. He could live on nothing, and at times, it was said, had done so. For his hardiness was great, and habitually he ate almost nothing. Man, God, and weather could not harm him. Of course he was sometimes put upon, for he would not quarrel. For having treated him better than he appeared to have expected, some people could hardly forgive themselves until they learned to take it as creditable. One tremendous tradesman, for instance, explained his comparative civility to Aurelius on a trying occasion by blustering: "You never know where you are with these Gypsies:" he came, however, to regard himself as a benefactor. A minister of the gospel who was tricked by Aurelius' innocence had to fall back on accusing him of concealing his age and of being a Welshman. Everyone thought him a foreigner.

It was a remarkable thing that nobody except a few children and Mr Torrance the schoolmaster—for actually one schoolmaster frequented Abercorran House—liked to be alone with Aurelius. I never heard this spoken of, and I believe nobody consciously avoided being alone with him. Only, it so happened that he was welcomed by a company, but not one member of it was likely to stay on long if at last he found himself and Aurelius left behind by the others. Meeting him in the street, no one ever stopped for more than a few words with him. Some awkwardness was feared, but not in Aurelius, who was never awkward. Unsympathetic people called him a foreigner, and there was something in it. In no imaginable crowd could he have been one of the million "friends, Romans, countrymen!" Perhaps even at Abercorran House he was not quite one of us. Yet in a moment he was at home there. I can see him holding a pigeon—in the correct manner—spreading out one of its wings and letting it slip back again, while he was talking, as luck would have it, to Higgs the bird-chap who cared for nothing but pigeons. Higgs was so taken aback by the way the new-comer talked and held the bird—a man whom he would instinctively have laughed at—that he could not say a word, but escaped as soon as possible and blundered about saying: "I like the little chap. . . . You can see he's used to birds—who would have thought it?—and I wondered what it was young Arthur was bringing in." Higgs was so pleased with his own discernment, his cleverness in seeing good in that unlikely place, that he really exaggerated his liking for Aurelius. However, let it be set down to Higgs' credit that he knew a hawk from a handsaw, and hailed Aurelius almost at first sight.

As I have mentioned, Aurelius had asked me to take him to Abercorran House, because I had attracted his fancy with something I had said about the Morgans or the house. It was a lucky introduction. For all liked him, and he was soon free to stay at the house for a night or a month, at pleasure. It was one of his virtues to admire Jessie. He must have felt at once that she was alone among women, since he never knelt to her or made any of his long, lofty speeches to her as to other fair women whom he met elsewhere, as at my home. She saw his merit instantly. To please him she would go on and on singing for him "The Cuckoo," "Midsummer Maid," "Hob-y-deri-dando," "Crockamy Daisy Kitty-alone."

When for a time he was a bookseller's assistant in London, it was Jessie discovered him, as she was passing with her mother at night. She said he was standing outside like one of those young men in "The Arabian Nights" who open a stall in a market at Bagdad because they hope to capture someone long-lost or much-desired among their customers. But he soon wearied of dry goods, and was not seen after that for over a year, though Mr Torrance brought word that he had written from Dean Prior in Devonshire, where (he said) a great poet lived who would have been sorry to die in 1674 if he had known he was going to miss Aurelius by doing so. Which may be absurd, but Mr Torrance said it, and he knew both Herrick and Aurelius extremely well. He did try to explain the likeness, but to an audience that only knew Herrick as the author of "Bid me to live" and as an immoral clergyman, and at this distance of time I cannot reconstruct the likeness. But it may have been that Aurelius wrote verses which Mr Torrance, in the kindness of his heart, believed to resemble Herrick's. I know nothing of that. The nearest to poetry I ever saw of his was a pack of cards which he spent his life, off and on, in painting. Jessie was one of the Queens, and rightly so. That this pack was found in the cottage where he stayed before he finally disappeared, proves, to me at any rate, that he regarded this life as at an end.

CHAPTER VI

OUR COUNTRY

"It was a good day, Arthur, that first brought you to Abercorran House," said old Ann, as she went to the door to deliver the stray pigeon to its owner.

"Yes," I said, a little pathetically for Ann's taste and with thought too deep for tears, at least in her company. I looked round the kitchen, remembering the glory that was Abercorran . . . Philip . . . Jessie . . . Roland . . . Aurelius . . . It was no unselfish memory, for I wished with all my heart that I was fifteen again, that the month was April, the hour noon, and the scene the yard of Abercorran House with all the family assembled, all the dogs, Aurelius, and Mr Torrance (there being still some days left of the Easter holidays), yes, and Higgs also, and most certainly the respectable Mr Stodham.

"Yes, it was a good day," continued Ann, returning, "if it had not been for you we should never have known Aurelius."

This was so like the old Ann that I was delighted, with all my conceit. I remembered that first visit well, limping into the yard the day after the paper-chase, and seeing big Jack (aged then about twenty) and tall Roland (less than two years younger) discussing a greyhound with a blackguard in an orange neck-tie, Jessie (my own age) surrounded by pigeons, Mr Morgan and Mr Torrance at the top of the steps looking on, and away on the pond under the elms little Harry and Lewis crying for help to release their craft from the water-lilies of that perilous sea. When the limper was introduced as "Arthur," Mr Torrance said:

> "Not that same Arthur, that with spear in rest
> Shot through the lists at Camelot and charged
> Before the eyes of ladies and of kings,"

and Mr Morgan roared with laughter, as having no cigar he was free to do at the moment, and everyone else joined in except the Gypsy, who appeared to think he was the victim; such laughter was a command. Before the roar was over Ann came up to me and said: "Will you please to come into the kitchen. I have something for that poor leg of yours." Pity was worse than ever, but to escape the laughter, I followed her. "There you are," she said as we entered, pointing to a broad blackberry tart uncut, "that will do your leg good. It is between you and Philip." And with that she left me and at another door in came Philip, and though there was nothing wrong with his leg he enjoyed the tart as much as I did.

We were then friends of twenty-four hours standing, my age being ten, his twelve, and the time of the year an October as sweet as its name. We had been for six months together at the same school without speaking, until yesterday, the day of the paper-chase. After running and walking for more than two hours that sunny morning we found ourselves together, clean out of London and also out of the chase, because he had gone off on a false scent and because I ran badly.

I had never before been in that lane of larches. It was, in fact, the first time that I had got out of London into pure country on foot. I had been by train to sea-side resorts and the country homes of relatives, but this was different. I had no idea that London died in this way into the wild.

Out on the broad pasture bounded by a copse like a dark wall, rooks cawed in the oak-trees. Moorhens hooted on a hidden water behind the larches. At the end of a row of cottages and gardens full of the darkest dahlias was a small, gray inn called "The George," which my companion entered. He came out again in a minute with bread and cheese for two, and eating slowly but with large mouthfuls we strolled on, too busy and too idle to talk. Instead of larches horse-chestnuts overhung our road; in the glittering grass borders the dark fruit and the white pods lay bright. So as we ate we stooped continually for the biggest "conquers" to fill our pockets. Suddenly the other boy, musing and not looking at me, asked, "What's your name?" "Arthur Froxfield," I answered, pleased and

36

not at all surprised. "It doesn't suit you," he said, looking at me. "It ought to be John something—

> 'John, John, John,
> With the big boots on.'

You're tired."

I knew his name well enough, for at twelve he was the best runner in the school. Philip Morgan. . . . I do not suppose that I concealed my pride to be thus in his company.

For an hour we were separated; we hit upon the trail, and off he went without a word. At a limping trot I followed, but lost sight of Philip and soon fell back into a walk. I had, in fact, turned homewards when he overtook me; he had been forced to retrace his steps. I was by this time worn out, and should have given up but for my self-satisfaction at the long run and the pleasure of knowing that he did not mind my hanging on his arm as on we crawled. Thus at last after an age of sleepy fatigue I found myself at home. It had been arranged that on the next day I was to go round to Abercorran House.

Again and again Philip and I revisited that lane of larches, the long water-side copse, the oak wood out in the midst of the fields, and all the hedges, to find moorhen's eggs, a golden-crested wren's, and a thousand treasures, and felicity itself. Philip had known this country for a year or more; now we always went together. I at least, for a long time, had a strong private belief that the place had been deserted, overlooked, forgotten, that it was known only to us. It was not like ordinary country. The sun there was peculiarly bright. There was something unusual in the green of its grass, in the caw of its rooks in April, in the singing of its missel-thrushes on the little round islands of wood upon the ploughland. When later on I read about those "remote and holy isles" where the three sons of Ulysses and Circe ruled over the glorious Tyrrhenians, I thought, for some reason or another, or perhaps for no reason, of those little round islands of ash and hazel amidst the ploughland of Our Country, when I was ten and Philip twelve. If we left it unvisited for some

37

weeks it used to appear to our imaginations extraordinary in its beauty, and though we might be forming plans to go thither again before long, I did not fully believe that it existed—at least for others—while I was away from it. I have never seen thrushes' eggs of a blue equalling those we found there.

No wonder Our Country was supernaturally beautiful. It had London for a foil and background; what is more, on that first day it wore an uncommon autumnal splendour, so that I cannot hope to meet again such heavily gilded elms smouldering in warm, windless sunshine, nor such bright meadows as they stood in, nor such blue sky and such white billowy cloud as rose up behind the oaks on its horizon.

Philip knew this Our Country in and out, and though his opinion was that it was not a patch on the country about his old home at Abercorran, he was never tired of it. In the first place he had been introduced to it by Mr Stodham. "Mr Stodham," said Philip, "knows more about England than the men who write the geography books. He knows High Bower, where we lived for a year. He is a nice man. He has a horrible wife. He is in an office somewhere, and she spends his money on jewellery. But he does not mind; remember that. He has written a poem and father does not want him to recite it. Glory be to Mr Stodham. When he trespasses they don't say anything, or if they do it is only, 'Fine day, sir,' or 'Where did you want to go to, sir,' or 'Excuse me, sir, I don't mind your being on my ground, but thought you mightn't be aware it is private.' But if they catch you or me, especially you, being only eleven and peagreen at that, we shall catch it."

Once he was caught. He was in a little copse that was all blackthorns, and the blackthorns were all spikes. Inside was Philip looking for what he could find; outside, and keeping watch, sat I; and it was Sunday. Sunday was the only day when you ever saw anyone in Our Country. Presently a man who was passing said: "The farmer's coming along this road, if that's any interest to you." It was too late. There he was—coming round the bend a quarter of a mile off, on a white pony. I whistled to Philip to look out. I was innocently sitting in the same place when the farmer rode up. He asked me at once the name of the boy in the copse, which so took me by surprise that I blabbed out at once. "Philip Morgan," shouted the farmer, "Philip Morgan, come out of that copse." But Philip was already out of it, as I guessed presently when I saw a labourer running towards the far end, evidently in pursuit. The farmer rode on, and thinking he had given it up I followed him. However, five minutes later Philip ran into his arms at a gateway, just as he was certain he had escaped, because his pursuer had been outclassed and had given up running. In a few minutes I joined them Philip was recovering his breath and at the same time giving his address. If we sent in five shillings to a certain hospital in his name, said the farmer, he would not prosecute us—"No," he added, "ten shillings, as it is Sunday." "The better the day the better the deed," said Philip scornfully. "Thank you, my lad," said the giver of charity, and so we parted. But neither did we pay the money, nor were we prosecuted; for my father wrote a letter from his official address. I do not know what he said. In future, naturally, we gave some of our time and trouble to avoiding the white pony when we were in those parts. Not that he got on our nerves. We had no nerves. No: but we made a difference. Besides, his ground was really not in what we called Our Country, *par excellence*. Our own country was so free from molestation that I thought of it instantly when Aurelius read to me about the Palace of the Mountain of Clouds. A great king had asked his counsellors and his companions if they knew of any place that no one could invade, no one, either man or genie. They told him of the Palace of the Mountain of Clouds. It has been built by a genie who had fled from Solomon in rebellion. There he had dwelt until the end of his days. After him no one inhabited it; for it was separated by great distances and great enchantment from the rest of the world. No one went thither. It was surrounded by running water sweeter than honey, colder than snow, and by fruitful trees. And there in the Palace of the Mountain of Clouds the king might dwell in safety and solitude for ever and ever. . . .

In the middle of the oak wood we felt as safe and solitary as if we were lords of the Palace of the Mountain of Clouds. And so we were. For four years we lived charmed lives. For example, when we had manufactured a gun and bought a pistol, we crawled over the ploughed fields at twilight, and fired both at a flock of pewits. Yet neither birds nor poachers suffered. We climbed the trees for the nests of crows, woodpeckers, owls, wood-pigeons, and once for a kestrel's, as if they were all ours. We went everywhere. More than once we found outselves among the lawns and shrubberies of big houses which we had never suspected. This seems generally to have happened at twilight. As we never saw the same house twice the mysteriousness was increased. One of the houses was a perfect type of the dark ancient house in a forest. We came suddenly stumbling upon it among the oaks just before night. The walls were high and craggy, and without lights anywhere. A yew tree grew right up against it. A crow uttered a curse from the oak wood. And that house I have never seen again save in memory. There it remains, as English as Morland, as extravagantly wild as Salvator Rosa. That evening Philip must needs twang his crossbow at the crow—an impossible shot; but by the grace of God no one came out of the house, and at this distance of time it is hard to believe that men and women were actually living there.

Most of these estates had a pond or two, and one had a long one like a section of a canal. Here we fished with impunity and an untroubled heart, hoping for a carp, now and then catching a tench. But often we did not trouble to go so far afield. Our own neighbourhood was by no means unproductive, and the only part of it which was sacred was the Wilderness. None of the birds of the Wilderness ever suffered at our hands. Without thinking about it we refrained from fishing in the Wilderness pond, and I never saw anybody else do so except Higgs, but though it seemed to me like robbing the offertory Higgs only grinned. But other people's grounds were honoured in a different way. Private shrubberies became romantic at night to the trespasser. Danger doubled their shadows, and creeping amongst them we missed no ecstasy of which we were capable. The danger caused no conscious anxiety or fear, yet contrived to heighten the colour of such expeditions. We never had the least expectation of being caught. Otherwise we should have had more than a little fear in the January night when we went out after birds, armed with nets and lanterns. The scene was a region of meadows, waiting to be built on and in the meantime occupied by a few horses and cows, and a football and a lawn-tennis club. Up and down the hedges we went with great hopes of four and twenty blackbirds or so. We had attained a deep and thrilling satisfaction but not taken a single bird when we were suddenly aware of a deep, genial voice asking, "What's the game?" It was a policeman. The sight acted like the pulling of a trigger—off we sped. Having an advantage of position I was the first to leap the boundary hedge into the road, or rather into the ditch between hedge and road. Philip followed, but not the policeman. We both fell at the jump, Philip landing on top of me, but without damage to either. We reached home, covered in mud and secret glory, which made up for the loss of a cap and two lanterns. The glory lasted one day only, for on the next I was compelled to accompany my father to the police-station to inquire after the cap and lanterns. However, I had the honour of hearing the policeman say—though laughing—that we had taken the leap like hunters and given him no chance at all. This and the fact that our property was not recovered preserved a little of the glory.

In these meadows, in the grounds which their owners never used at night, and in Our Country, Philip and I spent really a great deal of time, fishing, birds-nesting, and trying to shoot birds with cross-bow, pistol, or home-made gun. There were intervals of school, and of football and cricket, but these in memory do not amount to more than the towns of England do in comparison with the country. As on the map the towns are but blots and spots on the country, so the school-hours were embedded, almost buried away, in the holidays, official, semi-official, and altogether unofficial. Philip and I were together during most of them; even the three principal long holidays of the year were often shared, either in Wales with some of Philip's people, or at Lydiard Constantine, in Wiltshire, with my aunt Rachel.

CHAPTER VII

WOOL-GATHERING AND LYDIARD CONSTANTINE

ONE day at Abercorran House I heard Aurelius, Mr Morgan, and Mr Torrance in the Library, talking about wool-gathering. "Since Jessie told us about that river in Essex with the Welsh name," said Mr Morgan, laughing, "we have travelled from Gwithavon to Battersea Park Road and a fishmonger's advertisement. Such are the operations of the majestic intellect. How did we get all that way? Do you suppose the cave-men were very different, except that they did not trouble about philology and would have eaten their philologers, while they did without fishmongers because fish were caught to eat, not to sell, in those days?"

"Well!" said Aurelius, "we could not live if we had nothing in common with the cave-men. A man who was a mere fishmonger or a mere philologer could not live a day without artificial aid. Scratch a philologer sufficiently hard and you will find a sort of a cave-man."

"I think," continued Mr Morgan, "that we ought to prove our self-respect by going soberly back on our steps to see what by-ways took us out of Gwithavon to this point."

"I'm not afraid of you at that game," said Aurelius. "I have often played it during church services, or rather after them. A church service needs no further defence if it can provide a number of boys with a chance of good wool-gathering."

"Very true," said Mr Torrance, who always agreed with Aurelius when it was possible. A fancy had struck him, and instead of turning it into a sonnet he said: "I like to think that the original wool-gatherers were men whose taste it was to wander the mountains and be before-hand with the nesting birds, gathering stray wool from the rocks and thorns, a taste that took them into all sorts

42

of wild new places without over-loading them with wool, or with profit or applause."

"Very pretty, Frank," said Aurelius, who had himself now gone wool-gathering and gave us the benefit of it. He told us that he had just recalled a church and a preacher whose voice used to enchant his boyhood into a half-dream. The light was dim as with gold dust. It was warm and sleepy, and to the boy all the other worshippers seemed to be asleep. The text was the three verses of the first chapter of Genesis which describe the work of creation on the fifth day. He heard the clergyman's voice murmuring, "Let the waters bring forth abundantly the moving creature that hath life, and fowl that may fly above the earth in the open firmament of heaven."

"That was enough," said Aurelius, "for me it was all the sermon. It summoned up before me a coast of red crags and a black sea that was white where the waves got lost in the long corridors between the crags. The moon, newly formed to rule the night, stood full, large, and white, at the top of the sky, which was as black as the sea and cloudless. And out of the water were rising, by twos and threes, but sometimes in multitudes like a cloud, the birds who were to fly in the open firmament of heaven. Out of the black waste emerged sea-birds, one at a time, their long white wings spread wide out at first, but then as they paused on the surface, uplifted like the sides of a lyre; in a moment they were skimming this way and that, and, rising up in circles, were presently screaming around the moon. Several had only risen a little way when, falling back into the sea, they vanished, there, as I supposed, destined by the divine purpose to be deprived of their wings and to become fish. Eagles as red as the encircling crags came up also, but always solitary; they ascended as upon a whirlwind in one or two long spirals and, blackening the moon for a moment, towered out of sight. The little singing birds were usually cast up in cloudlets, white and yellow and blue and dappled, and, after hovering uncertainly at no great height, made for the crags, where they perched above the white foam, piping, warbling, and twittering, after their own kinds, either singly or in concert. Ever and anon flocks of those who had soared now floated downward across the moon and went over my head with necks

43

outstretched, crying towards the mountains, moors, and marshes, or sloped still lower and alighted upon the water, where they screamed whenever the surface yawned at a new birth of white or many-coloured wings. Gradually the sea was chequered from shore to horizon with birds, and the sky was throbbing continually with others, so that the moon could either not be seen at all, or only in slits and wedges. The crags were covered, as if with moss and leaves, by lesser birds who mingled their voices as if it were a dawn of May. . . ."

In my turn I now went off wool-gathering, so that I cannot say how the fifth day ended in the fancy of Aurelius, if you call it fancy. It being then near the end of winter, that vision of birds set me thinking of the nests to come. I went over in my mind the eggs taken and to be taken by Philip and me at Lydiard Constantine. All of last year's were in one long box, still haunted by the cheapest scent of the village shop. I had not troubled to arrange them; there was a confusion of moor-hens' and coots' big freckled eggs with the lesser blue or white or olive eggs, the blotted, blotched, and scrawled eggs. For a minute they were forgotten during the recollection of a poem I had begun to copy out, and had laid away with the eggs. It was the first poem I had ever read and re-read for my own pleasure, and I was copying it out in my best hand-writing, the capitals in red ink. I had got as far as "Some mute inglorious Milton here may rest." I tried to repeat the verses but could not, and so I returned to the eggs. I thought of April when we should once again butt our way through thickets of stiff, bristling stems, through thorn and briar and bramble in the double hedges. We should find the thrushes' nests in a certain copse of oak and blackthorn where the birds used hardly anything but moss, and you could see them far off among the dark branches, which seldom had many leaves, but were furred over with lichens. We would go to all those little ponds shadowed by hazels close to the farms, where there was likely to be a solitary moorhen's home, and up into the pollard willow which once had four starling's eggs at the bottom of a long narrow pocket. In all those spring days we had no conscious aim but finding nests, and if we were not scrambling in a wood we walked with heads lifted up to the trees, turned aside to the hedges, or bent down to the grass or undergrowth. We were not curious about the eggs; questions of numbers of variation in size, shape or colour, troubled us but fitfully. Sun, rain, wind, deep mud, water over the boots and knees, scratches to arms, legs, and face, dust in the eyes, fear of gamekeepers and farmers, excitement, dizziness, weariness, all were summed up by the plain or marked eggs in the scent box; they were all that visibly remained of these things, and I valued them in the same way and for the same reason as the athlete valued the parsley crown. The winning of this one or that was recalled with regret, sometimes that I had taken more than I should have done from the same nest, sometimes that I had not taken as many as would have been excusable; I blushed with annoyance because we had not revisited certain nests which were unfinished or empty when we discovered them—the plough-boys doubtless had robbed them completely, or they had merely produced young birds. How careless the country boys were, putting eggs into their hats and often forgetting all about them, often breaking them wantonly. I envied them their opportunities and despised them for making so little use of them.

I thought of the flowers we tramped over, the smell and taste of cowslips and primroses, and various leaves, and of the young brier shoots which we chewed and spat out again as we walked. I do not know what Aurelius might have been saying, but I began to count up the Sundays that must pass before there would be any chance of finding rooks' eggs, not at Lydiard, but at the rookery nearest to Abercorran House. Thus I was reminded of the rookery in the half-dozen elms of a farm-house home field, close by the best fishing-place of all at Lydiard. There the arrow-headed reeds grew in thick beds, and the water looked extraordinarily mysterious on our side of them, as if it might contain fabulous fish. Only last season I had left my baited line out there while I slipped through the neighbouring hedge to look for a reed-bunting's nest; and when I returned I had to pull in an empty line which some monster had gnawed through, escaping with hooks and bait. I wonder Philip did not notice. It was just there, between the beds of arrow-head and that immense water dock on the brink. I vowed to try again. Everybody had seen the monster, or at least the swirl made as he struck out into the deeps at a passing tread. "As long as my arm, I daresay," said the carter, cracking his whip emphatically with a sort of suggestion that the fish was not to be caught by the like of us. Well, we shall see.

As usual the idea of fishing was connected with my aunt Rachel. There was no fishing worth speaking of unless we stayed with her in our holidays. The water in the ponds at Lydiard Constantine provoked magnificent hopes. I could have enjoyed fishing by those arrow-heads without a bait, so fishy did it look, especially on Sundays, when sport was forbidden:—it was unbearable to see that look and lack rod and line. The fascinating look of water is indescribable, but it enables me to understand how

> "Simple Simon went a-fishing
> For to catch a whale,
> But all the water he had got
> Was in his mother's pail."

I have seen that look in tiny ponds, and have fished in one against popular advice, only giving it up because I caught newts there and nothing else.

But to my wool-gathering. In the Library, with Aurelius talking, I could see that shadowed water beside the reeds and the float in the midst. In fact I always had that picture at my command. We liked the water best when it was quite smooth; the mystery was greater, and we used to think that we caught more fish out of it in this state. I hoped it would be a still summer, and warm. It was nearly three quarters of a year since last we were in that rookery meadow—eight months since I had tasted my aunt's doughy cake. I can see her making it, first stoning the raisins while the dough in a pan by the fire was rising; when she thought neither of us was looking she stoned them with her teeth, but this did not shock me, and now I come to think of it they were very white even teeth, not too large or too small, so that I wonder no man ever married her for them

46

alone. I am glad no man did marry her—at least, I was glad then. For she would probably have given up making doughy cakes full of raisins and spices, if she had married. I suppose that what with making cakes and wiping the dough off her fingers, and wondering if we had got drowned in the river, she had no time for lovers. She existed for those good acts which are mostly performed in the kitchen, for supplying us with lamb and mint sauce, and rhubarb tart with cream, when we came in from birds-nesting. How dull it must be for her, thought I, sitting alone there at Lydiard Constantine, the fishing over, the birds not laying yet, no nephews to be cared for, and therefore no doughy cakes, for she could not be so greedy as to make them for herself and herself alone. Aunt Rachel lived alone, when she was without us, in a little cottage in a row, at the edge of the village. Hers was an end house. The rest were neat and merely a little stained by age; hers was hidden by ivy, which thrust itself through the walls and up between the flagstones of the floor, flapped in at the windows, and spread itself so densely over the panes that the mice ran up and down it, and you could see their pale, silky bellies through the glass—often they looked in and entered. The ivy was full of sparrows' nests, and the neighbours were indignant that she would not have them pulled out; even we respected them.

To live there always, I thought, would be bliss, provided that Philip was with me, always in a house covered with ivy and conducted by an aunt who baked and fried for you and tied up your cuts, and would clean half a hundred perchlings for you without a murmur, though by the end of it her face and the adjacent windows were covered with the flying scales. "Why don't you catch two or three really big ones?" she would question, sighing for weariness, but still smiling at us, and putting on her crafty-looking spectacles. "Whew, if we could," we said one to another. It seemed possible for the moment; for she was a wonderful woman, and the house wonderful too, no anger, no sorrow, no fret, such a large fire-place, everything different from London, and better than anything in London except Abercorran House. The ticking of her three clocks was delicious, especially very early in the morning as you lay

47

awake, or when you got home tired at twilight, before lamps were lit. Everything had been as it was in Aunt Rachel's house for untold time; it was natural like the trees; also it was never stale; you never came down in the morning feeling that you had done the same yesterday and would do the same to-morrow, as if each day was a new, badly written line in a copy-book, with the same senseless words at the head of every page. Why couldn't we always live there? There was no church or chapel for us—Philip had never in his life been to either. Sunday at Lydiard Constantine was not the day of grim dulness when everyone was set free from work, only to show that he or she did not know what to do or not to do; if they had been chained slaves these people from Candelent Street and elsewhere could not have been stiffer or more savagely solemn.

Those adult people were a different race. I had no thought that Philip or I could become like that, and I laughed at them without a pang, not knowing what was to save Philip from such an end. How different from those people was my aunt, her face serene and kind, notwithstanding that she was bustling about all day and had trodden her heels down and had let her hair break out into horns and wisps.

I thought of the race of women and girls. I thought (with a little pity) that they were nicer than men. I would rather be a man, I mused, yet I was sure women were better. I would not give up my right to be a man some day; but for the present there was no comparison between the two in my affections; and I should not have missed a single man except Aurelius. Nevertheless, women did odd things. They always wore gloves when they went out, for example. Now, if I put gloves on my hands, it was almost as bad as putting a handkerchief over my eyes or cotton wool in my ears. They picked flowers with gloved hands. Certainly they had their weaknesses. But think of the different ways of giving an apple. A man caused it to pass into your hands in a way that made it annoying to give thanks; a woman gave herself with it, it was as if the apple were part of her, and you took it away and ate it in peace, sitting alone, thinking of nothing. A boy threw an apple at you as if he wanted to knock your teeth out with it, and, of course, you threw it back at him with the same intent; a girl gave it in such a way that you wanted to give it back, if you were not somehow afraid. I began thinking of three girls who all lived near my aunt and would do anything I wanted, as if it was not I but they that wanted it. Perhaps it was. Perhaps they wanted nothing except to give. Well, and that was rather stupid, too.

Half released from the spell by one of the voices in the Library, I turned to a dozen things at once—as what time it was, whether one of the pigeons would have laid its second egg by now, whether Monday's post would bring a letter from a friend who was in Kent, going about the woods with a gamekeeper who gave him squirrels, stoats, jays, magpies, an owl, and once a woodcock, to skin. I recalled the sweet smell of the squirrels; it was abominable to kill them, but I liked skinning them. . . . I turned to thoughts of the increasing row of books on my shelf. First came The Compleat Angler. That gave me a brief entry into a thinly populated world of men rising early, using strange baits, catching many fish, talking to milkmaids with beautiful voices and songs fit for them. The book—in a cheap and unattractive edition—shut up between its gilded covers a different, embalmed, enchanted life without any care. Philip and I knew a great deal of it by heart, and took a strong fancy to certain passages and phrases, so that we used to repeat out of all reason "as wholesome as a pearch of Rhine," which gave a perfect image of actual perch swimming in clear water down the green streets of their ponds on sunny days. . . . Then there were Sir Walter Scott's poems, containing the magic words—

"And, Saxon, I am Rhoderick Dhu."

Next, Robinson Crusoe, Grimm's Fairy Tales, the Iliad, a mass of almost babyish books, tattered and now never touched, and lastly The Adventures of King Arthur and the Round Table. I heard the Lady of the Lake say to Merlin (who had a face like Aurelius) "Inexorable man, thy powers are resistless": moonlit water overhung by mountains, and crags crowned by towers, boats with mysterious dark freight; knights taller than Roland, trampling and glittering; sorceries, battles, dragons, kings, and maidens, stormed or flitted through my mind, some only as words and phrases, some as pictures. It was a shadow entertainment, with an indefinable quality of remoteness tinged by the pale Arthurian moonlight and its reflection in that cold lake, which finally suggested the solid comfort of tea at my aunt's house, and thick slices, "cut ugly," of the doughy cake.

At this point Jessie came in to say that tea was ready. "So am I," said I, and we raced downstairs. Jessie won.

CHAPTER VIII

ABERCORRAN AND MORGAN'S FOLLY

ONCE or twice I joined Philip on a holiday in Wales, but not at Abercorran. It was years later that I found myself by chance at Abercorran and saw enough of it to spoil somewhat the beautiful fantastic geography learned from a thousand references by Philip, Jessie, and old Ann. The real place—as it may be seen by anyone who can pay the railway fare—is excellent, but I think I should never have gone there had I foreseen its effect on that old geography. Having seen the place with these eyes I cannot recover perfectly the original picture of the castle standing at the meet of two small rivers and looking over their wide estuary, between the precipices of enormous hills, to the sea; the tiny deserted quay, the broken cross on the open space glistening with ever-renewed cockle shells, below the castle; the long, stately street leading from the church down to the castle, named Queen Street because an English queen once rode down it; the castle owls and the inexhaustible variety and the everlasting motion of the birds of the estuary. To see it as the Morgans once made me see it you must be able to cover the broad waters with glistening white breasts, at the same moment that its twin precipices abide in gloom that has been from the beginning; you must hear an undertone of the age of Arthur, or at least of the great Llewelyn, in the hoots of the castle owls, and give a quality of kingliness to a street which has a wide pavement on one side, it is true, but consists for the most part of cottages, with a castle low down at one end, and at the other a church high up.

The Morgans' old house, far above the townlet of Abercorran, had windows commanding mountains behind as well as sea in front. Their tales had given me, at the beginning, an idea of mountains, as distinct from those objects resembling saw teeth by which they are sometimes represented. They formed the foundation of my idea of mountains. Then upon that I raised slowly a magnificent edifice by means of books of travel and of romance. These later elements were also added unto the Welsh mountains where Jack found the kite's nest, where Roland saw an eagle, where Philip had learnt the ways of raven, buzzard, and curlew, of badger, fox, and otter. My notions of their size had been given to me by Ann, in a story of two men who were lost on them in the mist. For three days the men were neither seen nor heard in their wanderings; on the fourth they were discovered by chance, one dead, the other mad. These high solitudes, I thought, must keep men wild in their minds, and still more I thought so after hearing of the runaway boy from Ann's own parish. He lived entirely out of doors—without stealing, said Ann—for a year and a half. Every now and then someone caught sight of him, but that was all the news. He told nothing when he was arrested on the charge of setting fire to a rick. Ann said that if he did this it was an accident, but they wanted to get rid of the scandal of the "wild boy," so they packed him off to a training ship until he was sixteen. "He would have thought it a piece of luck," said Ann, "to escape from the ship, however it was, for he thought it worse than any weather on the mountains; and before he was sixteen he did escape—he fell overboard by some mercy, and was never seen again on sea or land, my children."

But above all other tales of the mountains was the one that had David Morgan for hero. David Morgan was the eldest brother of the Morgans of Abercorran House. He had been to London before ever the family thought of quitting their Welsh home; in a year's time he had returned with an inveterate melancholy. After remaining silent, except to his mother, for some months, he left home to build himself a house up in the mountains. When I was at Abercorran, Morgan's Folly—so everybody called it—was in ruins, but still made a black letter against the sky when the north was clear. People imagined that he had hidden gold somewhere among the rocks. He was said to have worshipped a god who never entered chapel or church. He was said to speak with raven and fox.

He was said to pray for the end of man or of the world. Atheist, blasphemer, outlaw, madman, brute, were some of the names he received in rumour. But the last that was positively known of him was that, one summer, he used to come down night after night, courting the girl Angharad who became his wife.

One of his obsessions in solitude, so said his mother when I travelled down with her to see the last of him, was a belief in a race who had kept themselves apart from the rest of men, though found among many nations, perhaps all. The belief may have come from the Bible, and this was the race that grew up alongside the family of Cain, the guiltless "daughters of men" from whom the children of the fratricides obtained their wives. These, untainted with the blood of Cain, knew not sin or shame—so his belief seems to have been—but neither had they souls. They were a careless and a godless race, knowing not good or evil. They had never been cast out of Eden. "In fact," said Mrs Morgan, "they must be something like Aurelius." Some of the branches of this race had already been exterminated by men; for example, the Nymphs and Fauns. David Morgan was not afraid of uttering his belief. Others of them, he said, had adopted for safety many of men's ways. They had become moorland or mountain men living at peace with their neighbours, but not recognised as equals. They were to be found even in the towns. There the uncommon beauty of the women sometimes led to unions of violent happiness and of calamity, and to the birth of a poet or musician who could abide neither with the strange race nor with the children of Adam. They were feared but more often despised, because they retained what men had lost by civilisation, because they lived as if time was not, yet could not be persuaded to believe in a future life.

Up in his tower Morgan came to believe his own father one of this people, and resolved to take a woman from amongst them for a wife. Angharad, the shy, the bold, the fierce dark Angharad whose black eyes radiated light and blackness together, was one of them. She became his wife and went up with him to the tower. After that these things only were certainly known; that she was unhappy; that when she came down to the village for food she was silent, and would never betray him or fail to return; and that he himself never came down, that he also was silent and with his unshorn hair looked like a wild man. He was seen at all hours, usually far off, on the high paths of the mountains. His hair was as black as in boyhood. He was never known to have ailed, until one day the wild wife knocked at a farmhouse door near Abercorran, asking for help to bring him where he might be looked after, since he would have no one in the tower but her. The next day Mrs Morgan travelled down to see her son. When she asked me to accompany her I did so with some curiosity; for I had already become something of a stranger at Abercorran House, and had often wondered what had become of David Morgan up on his tower. His mother talked readily of his younger days and his stay in London. Though he had great gifts, some said genius, which me might have been expected to employ in the study, he had applied himself to direct social work. For a year he laboured "almost as hard," he said, "as the women who make our shirts." But gradually he formed the opinion that he did not understand town life, that he never could understand the men and women whom he saw living a town life pure and simple. Before he came amongst them he had been thinking grandly about men without realising that these were of a different species. His own interference seemed to him impudent. They disgusted him, he wanted to make them more or less in his own image to save his feelings, which, said he, was absurd. He was trying to alter the conditions of other men's lives because he could not have himself endured them, because it would have been unpleasant to him to be like them in their hideous pleasure, hideous suffering, hideous indifference. In this attitude, which altogether neglected the consolations and even beauty and glory possible or incident to such a life, he saw a modern Pharisaism whose followers did not merely desire to be unlike others, but to make others like themselves. It was, he thought, due to lack of the imagination and sympathy to see their lives from a higher or a more intimate point of view, in connection with implicit ideals, not as a spectacle for which he had an expensive seat. Did they fall farther short of their ideals than he from his? He had not the power to see, but he thought not; and he came to believe that, lacking as their life might be in familiar forms of beauty and power, it possessed, nevertheless, a profound unconsciousness and dark strength which might some day bring forth beauty—might even now be beautiful to simple and true eyes—and had already given them a fitness to their place which he had for no place on earth. When it was food and warmth which were lacking he never hesitated to use his money, but beyond satisfying these needs he could not feel sure that he was not fancifully interfering with a force which he did not understand and could not overestimate. Therefore, leaving all save a little of his money to be spent in directly supplying the needs of hungry and cold men, he escaped from the sublime, unintelligible scene. He went up into the tower that he had built on a rock in his own mountains, to think about life before he began to live. Up there, said his mother, he hoped to learn why sometimes in a London street, beneath the new and the multitudinous, could be felt a simple and a pure beauty, beneath the turmoil a placidity, beneath the noise a silence which he longed to reach and drink deeply and perpetuate, but in vain. It was his desire to learn to see in human life, as we see in the life of bees, the unity, which perhaps some higher order of beings can see through the complexity which confuses us. He had set out to seek at first by means of science, but he thought that science was an end, not a means. For a hundred years, he said, men had been reading science and investigating, as they had been reading history, with the result that they knew some science and some history. "So he went up into his tower, and there he has been these twelve years," said Mrs Morgan, "with Angharad and no comforts. You would think by his letters that his thoughts had become giddy up there. Only five letters have I had from him in these twelve years. This is all," she added, showing a small packet in her handbag. "For the last six years nobody has heard from him except Ann. He wished he had asked Ann to go with him to the tower. She would have gone, too. She would have preserved him from being poetical. It is true he was only twenty-five years old at the time, but he was too poetical. He said things which he was bound to repent in a year, perhaps in a day. He writes quite seriously, as actors half seriously talk, in tones quite in-humanly sublime." She read me scraps from these old letters, evidently admiring as well as disapproving:

"I am alone. From my tower I look out at the huge desolate heaves of the grey beacons. Their magnitude and pure form give me a great calm. Here is nothing human, gentle, disturbing, as there is in the vales. There is nothing but the hills and the silence, which is God. The greater heights, set free from night and the mist, look as if straight from the hands of God, as if here He also delighted in pure form and magnitude that are worthy of His love. The huge shadows moving slowly over the grey spaces of winter, the olive spaces of summer, are as God's hand. . . .

"While I watch, the dream comes, more and more often, of a Paradise to be established upon the mountains when at last the wind shall blow sweet over a world that knows not the taint of life any more than of death. Then my thought sweeps rejoicing through the high Gate of the Winds that cleaves the hills—you could see it from my bedroom at Abercorran—far off, where a shadow miles long sleeps across the peaks, but leaves the lower wild as yellow in the sunlight as corn. . . .

"Following my thought I have walked upwards to that Gate of the Winds, to range the high spaces, sometimes to sleep there. Or I have lain among the gorse—I could lie on my back a thousand years, hearing the cuckoo in the bushes and looking up at the blue sky above the mountains. In the rain and wind I have sat against one of the rocks in the autumn bracken until the sheep have surrounded me, shaggy and but half visible through the mist, peering at me fearlessly, as if they had not seen a man since that one was put to rest under the cairn above; I sat on and on in the mystery, part of it but not divining, so that I went disappointed away. The crags stared at me on the hill-top where the dark spirits of the earth had crept out of their abysses into the day, and, still clad in darkness, looked grimly at the sky, the light, and at me. . . .

"More and more now I stay in the tower, since even in the mountains as to a greater extent in the cities of men, I am dismayed by numbers, by variety, by the grotesque, by the thousand gods demanding idolatry instead of the One I desire, Whose hand's shadow I have seen far off. . . .

"Looking on a May midnight at Algol rising from behind a mountain, the awe and the glory of that first step into the broad heaven exalted me; a sound arose as of the whole of Time making music behind me, a music as of something passing away to leave me alone in the silence, so that I also were about to step off into the air. . . ."

"Oh," said Mrs Morgan, "it would do him good to do something—to keep a few pigeons, now. I am afraid he will take to counting the stones in his tower." She continued her quotations:

"The moon was rising. The sombre ranges eastward seemed to be the edge of the earth, and as the orb ascended, the world was emptied and grieved, having given birth to this mighty child. I was left alone. The great white clouds sat round about on the horizon, judging me. For days I lay desolate and awake, and dreamed and never stirred."

"You see," said Mrs Morgan, "that London could not cure him. He says:

"'I have visited London. I saw the city pillared, above the shadowy abyss of the river, on columns of light; and it was less than one of my dreams. It was Winter and I was resolved to work again in Poplar. I was crossing one of the bridges, full of purpose and thought, going against the tide of the crowd. The morning had a low yellow roof of fog. About the heads of the crowd swayed a few gulls, inter-lacing so that they could not be counted. They swayed like falling snow and screamed. They brought light on their long wings, as the ship below, setting out slowly with misty masts, brought light to the green and leaden river upon the foam at her bows. And ever about the determined, careless faces of the men swayed the pale wings, like wraiths of evil and good, calling and calling to ears that know not what they hear. And they tempted my brain with the temptation of their beauty: I went to and fro to hear and to see them until they slept and the crowd had flowed away. I rejoiced that day, for I thought that this beauty had made ready my brain, and that on the mountains at last I should behold the fulness and the simplicity of beauty. So I went away without seeing Poplar. But there, again, among the mountains was weariness, because I also was there.'"

"Why is he always weary?" asked Mrs Morgan plaintively, before reading on:

"But not always weariness. For have I not the company of planet and star in the heavens, the same as bent over prophet, poet, and philosopher of old? By day a scene unfolds as when the first man spread forth his eyes and saw more than his soul knew. These things lift up my heart sometimes for days together, so that the voices of fear and doubt are not so much in that infinite silence as rivulets in an unbounded plain. The sheer mountains, on some days, seem to be the creation of my own lean terrible thoughts, and I am glad: the soft, wooded hills below and behind seem the creation of the pampered luxurious thought which I have left in the world of many men. . . .

"Would that I could speak in the style of the mountains. But language, except to genius and simple men, is but a paraphrase, dissipating and dissolving the forms of passion and thought. . . .

"Again Time lured me back out of Eternity, and I believed that I longed to die as I lay and watched the sky at sunset inlaid with swart forest, and watched it with a dull eye and a cold heart. . . ."

"And they think he is an atheist. They think he has buried gold on the mountain," exclaimed Mrs Morgan, indignantly.

Little she guessed of the nights before her in the lone farmhouse with her bewildered son and the wild Angharad. While he raved through his last hours and Angharad spent herself in wailing, and Mrs Morgan tried to steady his thoughts, I could only walk about the hills. I climbed to the tower, but learnt nothing because Morgan or his wife had set fire to it on leaving, and the shell of stones only remained.

On the fourth morning, after a night of storm, all was over. That morning once more I could hear the brook's murmur which had been obliterated by the storm and by thought. The air was clear and gentle in the coomb behind the farm, and all but still after the night of death and of great wind. High up in the drifting rose of dawn the tall trees were swaying their tips as if stirred by memories of the tempest. They made no sound in the coomb with the trembling of their slender length; some were never to sound again, for they lay motionless and prone in the underwood, or hung slanting among neighbour branches, where they fell in the night— the rabbits could nibble at crests which once wavered about the stars. The path was strewn with broken branches and innumerable twigs.

The silence was so great that I could hear, by enchantment of the ears, the departed storm. Yet the tragic repose was unbroken. One robin singing called up the roars and tumults that had to cease utterly before his voice could gain this power of peculiar sweetness and awe and make itself heard.

The mountains and sky, beautiful as they were, were more beautiful because a cloak of terror had been lifted from them and left them free to the dark and silver, and now rosy, dawn. The masses of the mountains were still heavy and sombre, but their ridges and the protruding tower bit sharply into the sky; the uttermost peaks appeared again, dark with shadows of clouds of a most lustrous whiteness that hung like a white forest, very far off, in the country of the sun. Seen out of the clear gloom of the wood this country was as a place to which a man might wholly and vainly desire to go, knowing that he would be at rest there and there only.

As I listened, walking the ledge between precipice and precipice in the coomb, the silence murmured of the departed tempest like a seashell. I could hear the dark hills convulsed with a hollow roaring as of an endless explosion. All night the trees were caught up and shaken in the furious air like grasses; the sounds on earth were mingled with those of the struggle in the high spaces of air. Outside the window branches were brandished wildly, and their anger was the more terrible because the voice of it could not be distinguished amidst the universal voice. The sky itself seemed to aid the roar, as the stars raced over it among floes of white cloud, and dark menacing fragments flitted on messages of darkness across the white. I looked out from the death room, having turned away from the helpless, tranquil bed and the still wife, and saw the hillside trees surging under a wild moon, but they were strange and no longer to be recognised, while the earth was heaving and be-nightmared by the storm. It was the awe of that hour which still hung over the coomb, making its clearness so solemn, it silence so pregnant, its gentleness so sublime. How fresh it was after the sick room, how calm after the vain conflict with death.

The blue smoke rose straight up from the house of death, over there in the white fields, where the wife sat and looked at the dead. Everyone else was talking of the strange life just ended, but the woman who had shared it would tell nothing; she wished only to persuade us that in spite of his extraordinary life he was a good man and very good to her. She had become as silent as Morgan himself, though eleven years before, when she began to live with him on the mountain, she was a happy, gay woman, the best dancer and singer in the village, and had the most lovers. Upon the mountain her wholly black Silurian eyes had turned inwards and taught her lips their mystery and Morgan's. They buried him, according to his wish, at the foot of the tower. Outraged by this, some of the neighbours removed his body to the churchyard under the cover of night. Others equally enraged at putting such a one in consecrated ground, exhumed him again. But in the end it was in the churchyard that his bones came to rest, with the inscription, chosen by Ann:

"Though thou shouldest make thy nest as high as the eagle,
I will bring thee down from thence, saith the Lord."

Angharad married a pious eccentric much older than herself, and in a year inherited his money. She lives on in one of those gray houses which make Queen Street so stately at Abercorran. She keeps no company but that of the dead. The children call her Angharad of the Folly, or simply Angharad Folly.

"She ought to have gone back to the tower," said Mr Torrance in some anger.

"She would have done, Mr Torrance," said Ann, "if she had been a poet; but you would not have done it if you had been through those eleven years and those four nights. No, I really don't think you would. . . . I knew a poet who jumped into a girl's grave, but he was not buried with her. Now you are angry with him, poor fellow, because he did not insist on being buried. Well, but it is lucky he was not, because if he had been we should not have known he was a poet."

"Well said, Ann," muttered Aurelius.

"Ann forgets that she was young once," protested Mr Torrance.

"No," she said, "I don't think I do, but I think this, that you forget you will some day be old. Now, as this is Shrove Tuesday and you will be wanting pancakes I must go make them."

"Good old Ann," whispered Mr Torrance.

CHAPTER IX

MR TORRANCE THE CHEERFUL MAN

MR TORRANCE openly objected to Ann's epitaph for David Morgan, preferring his own choice of one from Shelley's "Mont Blanc":

> "And what were thou, and earth, and stars, and sea,
> If to the human mind's imaginings
> Silence and solitude were vacancy?"

"But" said Mr Morgan, "Shelley was born only a hundred years ago, and died at thirty, I think that in the matter of mountains an older man is better."

"But, father," said Roland, "how do you know that Jeremiah was not drowned at thirty with a copy of 'Ecclesiastes' clasped to his bosom?"

"You read and see, my son," answered Mr Morgan. "Shelley could not pass himself off as an old man, though you know he did once claim to be eighty-nine, and Jeremiah would not have pretended to be thirty. That is only my opinion. I prefer the prophet, like Ann."

Mr Torrance muttered that anyone who preferred Jeremiah to Shelley had no right to an opinion. It was just like Mr Torrance. He was always saying foolish things and fairly often doing them, and yet we felt, and Mr Morgan once declared, that he had in him the imperishable fire of a divine, mysterious wisdom. After walking the full length of the Abbey Road, where he lived, to discover him smiling in his dark study, was sufficient proof that he had a wisdom past understanding.

Abbey Road was over two miles long. At its south end was a double signboard, pointing north "To London," south "To Forden, Field, and Cowmore"; at its north end it ran into pure London. Every year the horse-chestnut branches had to be shortened in May because their new leaf smothered the signboard. As if anyone who had reached that point could wish to be directed to London! Almost as few could wish to know the way in order to avoid it. But the horse-chestnut had to suffer. It was fortunate in not being cut down altogether and carried away. The cemetery saved it. The acute angle between the Abbey Road and another was filled by a large new cemetery, and the tree was the first of a long line within its railings. Even had the signboard been on the other side of the road it would have been as badly off among the tall thorns and stunted elms of the hedges. Behind this hedge was a waste, wet field, grazed over by a sad horse or two all through the year; for on account partly of the cemetery, partly of the factory which manufactured nobody quite knew what except stench, this field could not be let or sold. Along its far side ran a river which had no sooner begun to rejoice in its freedom to make rush and reed at pleasure on the border of the field than it found itself at the walls of the factory. Northward, past the cemetery and the factory, began the houses of Abbey Road, first a new house, occupied but with a deserted though not wild garden, and next to it a twin house, left empty. Then followed a sluttery of a few pairs or blocks of small houses, also new, on both sides of the road—new and yet old, with the faces of children who are smeared, soiled, and doomed, at two. They bordered on the old inn, "The Woodman's Arms," formerly the first house, having a large kitchen garden, and masses of dahlias and sunflowers behind. It lay back a good space from the road, and this space was gravel up to the porch, and in the middle of it stood a stone drinking trough. Often a Gypsy's cart and a couple of long dogs panting in the sun were to be seen outside, helping the inn to a country look, a little dingy and decidedly private and homely, so that what with the distance between the road and the front door, and the Gypsy's cart, the passer-by was apt to go on until he came to an ordinary building erected for the sale of beer and spirits, and for nothing else. Such a one lay not much further on, beyond a row of cottages contemporary with "The Woodman's Arms." These had long narrow gardens behind wooden posts and rails—gardens where everything tall, old-fashioned, and thick grew at their own sweet will, almost hiding the cottages of wood covered in creeper. You could just see that some were empty, their windows smashed or roughly boarded up, and that others were waiting for some old woman to die before they also had their windows smashed or boarded up. The dahlias, the rose-of-Sharon, the sweet rocket, the snow-on-the-mountains, the nasturtiums, the sunflowers, flourished too thick for weeds to make headway, and so probably with small help from the inhabitants, the gardens earned many a wave of the whip from passing drivers. The row of cottages meant "the first bit of country," with a sweep at one end, a rat-catcher at the other, announced in modest lettering. Between the last of them and the new public-house a puddled lane ran up along old and thick, but much broken, hedges to the horse-slaughterer's. "The Victoria Hotel" was built in the Jubilee year of that sovereign, and was a broad-faced edifice of brick with too conspicuous stone work round the windows and doorways and at the corners. The doors were many and mostly of glass. The landlord of "The Victoria" had no time to stand on his doorstep—whichever was his—like the landlord of "The Woodman"; moreover, all his doorsteps were right on the road, and he could have seen only the long row of cottages, by the same builder, which looked as if cut off from a longer, perhaps an endless row, with a pair of shears; while from the old inn could be seen grass sloping to the willows of the river, and a clump of elms hiding the factory chimneys. All the glass and brass of the "Victoria" shone spotless as if each customer out of the regiments in the crowded straight streets gave it a rub on entering and leaving.

Beyond the "Victoria" the road straightened itself after a twist, and was now lined by a hundred houses of one pattern but broken by several branch streets. These were older houses of grey stucco, possessing porches, short flights of steps up to the doors, basements, and the smallest of front gardens packed with neglected laurel, privet, marigold, and chickweed. At the end of the hundred—at No. 367—a man walking "To London" would begin to feel tired, and would turn off the pavement into the road, or else cross to the other side where the scattered new shops and half-built houses had as yet no footway except uneven bare earth. On this side the turnings were full of new houses and pavements, and admitted the eye to views of the welter of slate roofs crowding about the artificial banks of the river which ran as in a pit. Of the branch streets interrupting the stucco hundred, one showed a wide, desolate, untouched field of more and more thistles in the middle, more and more nettles at the edge, and, facing it, a paltry miracle of brand-new villas newly risen out of a similar field; the second was the straight line of a new street, with kerb-stones neat and new, but not a house yet among the nettles; another, an old lane, was still bordered by tender-leafed lime trees, preserved to deck the gardens of houses to come. The lane now and then had a Gypsy's fire in it for a few hours, and somebody had told the story that Aurelius was born under one of the trees; to which Aurelius answered, "The trees and I were born about the same time, but a hundred miles apart."

The stucco line gave way to a short row of brick houses, low and as plain as possible, lying well back from the road behind their split-oak fences, thorn hedges, laburnums and other fancy trees. Ivy climbed over all; each was neat and cheerful, but the group had an exclusive expression. Yet they had to look upon half-built shops and houses, varied by a stretch of tarred and barbed fence protecting the playing ground of some football club, whose notice board stood side by side with an advertisement of the land for building on leasehold; over the fence leaned an old cart-horse with his hair between his eyes.

There followed repetitions and variations of these things— inhabited houses, empty houses, houses being erected, fields threatened by houses—and finally a long, gloomy unbroken cliff of stained stucco. The tall houses, each with a basement and a long flight of steps up to a pillared porch, curved away to the number 593, and the celebrated "Horse-shoe Hotel" next door, which looked with dignity and still more ostentation, above its potted bay-trees, on the junction of Abbey Road and two busy thoroughfares. Opposite the tall stucco cliff a continuous but uneven line of newish mean shops of every kind and not more than half the height of the private houses, curved to a public-house as large as the "Horse-shoe" which it faced.

As each rook knows its nest among the scores on the straight uniform beeches, so doubtless each inhabitant could after a time distinguish his own house in this monotonous series, even without looking at the number, provided that there was light and that he was not drunk. Each house had three storeys, the first of them bay-windowed, above the basement. Probably each was divided between two, or, like No. 497, between three, families. Who had the upper storeys I never knew, except that there was an old woman who groaned on the stairs, a crying baby and its mother, and some men. I heard them speak, or cry, or tread the stairs lightly or heavily, but never happened to see any of them, unless that woman was one who was going to enter the gate at the same time as I one evening, but at the sight of me went past with a jug of something half hid under her black jacket. The basement, the floor above, and the garden, were rented to one family, viz., Mr Torrance, his wife and four children.

The garden was a square containing one permanent living thing, and one only, an apple tree which bore large fluted apples of palest yellow on the one bough remaining green among the grey barkless ones. All round the tree the muddy gravel had been trodden, by children playing, so hard that not a weed or blade of grass ever pierced it. Up to it and down to it led two narrow and steep flights of steps, the lower for the children and the mother ascending from the kitchen or living room, the upper for Mr Torrance who used to sit in the back room writing books, except in the mornings when he taught drawing at several schools. He wrote at an aged and time-worm black bureau, from which he could sometimes see the sunlight embracing the apple tree. But into that room the sunlight could not enter without a miracle, or by what so seldom happened as to seem one—the standing open of an opposite window just so that it threw a reflection of the late sun for about three minutes. Even supposing that the sunlight came that

66

way, little could have penetrated that study; for the French windows were ponderously draped by tapestry of dark green with a black pattern, and on one side the bureau, on the other a bookcase, stood partly before the panes. No natural light could reach the ceiling or the corners. Instead of light, books covered the walls, books in a number of black-stained bookcases of various widths, all equal in height with the room, except one that was cut short by a grate in which I never saw a fire. The other few interspaces held small old pictures or prints in dark frames, and a dismal canvas darkened, probably, by some friendly hand. Most of the books were old, many were very old. The huge, blackened slabs of theology and drama emitted nothing but gloom. The red bindings which make some libraries tolerable had been exorcised from his shelves by the spirits of black and of darkest brown.

The sullen host of books left little room for furniture. Nevertheless, there was a massive table of ancient oak, always laden with books, and apparently supported by still other books. Six chairs of similar character had long succeeded in retaining places in front of the books, justifying themselves by bearing each a pile or a chaos of books. Dark as wintry heather were the visible portions of the carpet. The door was hung with the same black and green tapestry as the windows; if opened, it disclosed the mere blackness of a passage crowded with more books and ancestral furniture.

Yet Mr Torrance smiled whenever a visitor, or his wife, or one or all of his children, but, above all, when Aurelius entered the room. No doubt he did not always smile when he was alone writing; for he wrote what he was both reluctant and incompetent to write, at the request of a firm of publishers whose ambition was to have a bad, but nice-looking, book on everything and everybody, written by some young university man with private means, by some vegetarian spinster, or a doomed hack like Mr Torrance. Had he owned copies of all these works they would have made a long row of greens and reds decorated by patterns and lettering in gold. He did not speak of his work, or of himself, but listened, smiled, or—with the children—laughed, and allowed himself at worst the remark that things were not so bad as they seemed. He was full of laughter, but all clever people thought him devoid of humour. In his turn, he admired all clever people, but was uninfluenced by them, except that he read the books which they praised and at once forgot them—he had read Sir Thomas Browne's "Quincunx," but could not say what a Quincunx was. Aurelius used to tease him some-times, I think, in order to prove that the smile was invincible. Mr Torrance was one of the slowest and ungainliest of men, but he was never out of love or even out of patience with Aurelius, the most lightsome of men, or of the superfluous race. He had fine wavy hair like silk fresh from the cocoon, and blue eyes of perfect innocence and fearlessness placed well apart in a square, bony, and big-nosed face that was always colourless. As he wrote, one or all of the children were likely to cry until they were brought into his study, where he had frequently to leave them to avoid being submerged in the chaos set moving by their play. He smiled at it, or if he could not smile, he laughed. If the children were silent for more than a little time he would go out into the passage and call downstairs to make sure that all was well, whereupon at least one must cry, and his wife must shriek to him in that high, sour voice which was always at the edge of tears. Often she came before he called, to stand at his door, talking, complaining, despairing, weeping; and though very sorry, Mr Torrance smiled, and as soon as she had slammed the door he went on with his exquisite small hand-writing, or, at most, he went out and counted the apples again. One or more of the children was always ill, nor was any ever well. They were untidy, graceless, and querulous, in looks resembling their mother, whose face seemed to have grown and shaped itself to music—a music that would set the teeth of a corpse on edge. She was never at the end of her work, but often of her strength. She was cruel to all in her impatience, and in her swift, giddy remorse cruel to herself also. She seemed to love and enjoy nothing, yet she would not leave the house on any account, and seldom her work. Whatever she did she could not ruffle her husband or wring from him anything but a smile and a slow, kind sentence. Not that he was content, or dull, or made of lead or wood. He would have liked to dress his wife and children as prettily as they could choose, to ride easily everywhere, anywhere, all over the world if it pleased them, seeing, hearing, tasting nothing but what they thought best on earth. But save in verse he never did so. It was one of his pains that seldom more than once or twice a year came the mood for doing what seemed to him the highest he could, namely, write verses. Also he had bad health; his pipe, of the smallest size, half filled with the most harmless and tasteless tobacco, lay cold on the bureau, just tasted and then allowed to go out. Ale he loved, partly for its own sake, partly to please Aurelius, but it did not love him. It was one of the jokes concerning him, that he could not stand the cold of his morning bath unless he repeated the words,

> "Up with me, up with me, into the sky,
> For thy song, lark, is strong."

He said them rapidly, and in an agony of solemnity, as he squeezed the sponge, and though this fact had become very widely known indeed, he did not give up the habit. Had he given up every kind of food condemned by himself or his doctors, he would have lived solely on love in that dark, that cold, that dead room. He was fond of company, but he knew nobody in all those thronged streets, unless it was an old woman or two, and their decrepit, needy husbands. He was a farmer's son, and knew little more of London than Ann, since he had moved into Abbey Road shortly after his first child was born, and had not been able to extricate himself from the books and furniture.

I see him, as soon as I have sat down by the window, swing round in his chair and look grim as he lights his tobacco with difficulty—then smile and let the smoke pour out of his mouth before beginning to talk, which means that in a few minutes he has laid down the pipe unconsciously, and that it will remain untouched. The children come in; he opens the French windows, and goes down the steps to the apple tree, carrying half the children, followed by the other half. Up he climbs, awkwardly in his black clothes, and getting that grim look under the strain, but smiling at last. He picks all of the seven apples and descends with them. The children are perfectly silent. "This one," he begins, "is for Annie because she is so small. And this for Jack because he is a good boy. And this for Claude because he is bad and we are all sorry for him. And this for Dorothy because she is so big." He gives me one, and Dorothy another to take down to her mother, and the last he stows away.

Mr Torrance was often fanciful, and as most people said, affected, in speech. He was full of what appeared to be slight fancies that made others blush uncomfortably. He had rash admirations for more conspicuously fanciful persons, who wore extraordinary clothes or ate or drank in some extraordinary manner. He never said an unkind thing. By what aid, in addition to the various brown breads to which he condemned himself, did he live, and move, and have his being with such gladness?

His books are not the man. They are known only to students at the British Museum who get them out once and no more, for they discover hasty compilations, ill-arranged, inaccurate, and incomplete, and swollen to a ridiculous size for the sake of gain. They contain not one mention of the house under the hill where he was born.

CHAPTER X

THE HOUSE UNDER THE HILL

Though he did not write of it, Mr Torrance would gladly talk of the house under the hill where he was born, of the surrounding country and its people. "I can only hope," he would say, "I can only hope that when I am old, 'in this our pinching cave,' I shall remember chiefly the valley of the river Uther where I was born, and the small old house half encircled and half-shadowed by an emormous crescent of beech-covered hills. That is my world in spite of everything. Those fifteen or twenty square miles make the one real thing that I know and cannot forget, in spite of a hundred English scenes wantonly visited and forgotten, in spite of London unforgotten and unintelligible.

"A brook ran out of the hills where they were nearest to us, about half a mile away. Dark trees darkened the two springs of crystal, and the lightest wind made a sad sound in the leaves above them. Before it had travelled a quarter of a mile the brook had gathered about itself a brotherhood of huge trees that always seemed to belong to it, and gave it pomp and mystery together, if the combination is possible. These were sunny trees, a line of towering tall black poplars that led out from the hills to the open agricultural land, a group of the mightiest wych-elms I have ever seen, and one ash-tree standing alone at the water's edge, the only one of its kind in the neighbourhood. Three miles from its source the brook ran into the main stream of the river Uther, and beyond that I knew nothing except by rumour and guessing. A line drawn between the two ends of the crescent of hills would pass through the junction of brook and river and enclose the country which was mine entirely. The long line of hills far off on the other side of the valley—bare, rounded, and cloud-like hills, whose curving ridges seemed to have growth and change like clouds—was the boundary of the real world, beyond which lay the phantasmal—London, the ocean, China, the Hesperides, Wineland, and all the islands and all the lands that were in books and dreams.

"The farm-houses of my country, and also the manor-house, stood on either side of the brook, low down. There was a mill and a chain of ponds, hardly a mile from the source. Both the ponds and the running water were bordered thickly with sedge, which was the home of birds far more often heard than seen.

"The Brook wound among little hills which were also intersected by rough roads, green lanes, footpaths, and deserted trackways, watery, and hollow and dark. As the roads never went on level ground all were more or less deeply worn, and the overhanging beeches above and the descending naked roots made them like groves in a forest. When a road ran into another or crossed it there was a farm. The house itself was of grey-white stone, roofed with tiles; the barn and sheds, apparently tumbling but never tumbledown, were of dark boards and thatch, and surrounded by a disorderly region of nettles, remains of old buildings and walls, small ponds either black in the shadow of quince bushes, or emerald with duck-weed, and a few big oaks or walnuts where the cart-horses and their foals and a young bull or two used to stand. A moorhen was sure to be swimming across the dark pond with a track of ripples like a peacock's tail shining behind it. Fowls scuttered about or lay dusting themselves in the middle of the road, while a big black-tailed cock perched crowing on a plough handle or a ruined shed. A cock without a head or a running fox stood up or drooped on the roof for a weather-vane, but recorded only the wind of some long past year which had finally disabled it. The walls of outhouses facing the road were garrulous with notices of sales and fairs to be held shortly or held years ago.

"At a point where one lane ran into another, as it were on an island, the inn with red blinds on its four windows looked down the road. The inn-keeper was a farmer by profession, but every day drank as much as he sold, except on a market or fair day. On an ordinary day I think he was always either looking down the road for someone to come and drink with him, or else consoling himself inside for lack of company. He seemed to me a nice man, but enormous; I always wondered how his clothes contained him; yet he could sit on the mower or tosser all day long in the June sun when he felt inclined. On a market or fair day there would be a flock of sheep or a lot of bullocks waiting outside while the drover smoked half a pipe and drank by the open door. And then the landlord was nowhere to be seen: I suppose he was at the market or up in the orchard. For it was the duty of his wife, a little mousy woman with mousy eyes, to draw the beer when a customer came to sit or stand among the empty barrels that filled the place. It was called 'The Crown.' They said it had once been 'The Crown and Cushion,' but the cushion was so hard to paint, and no one knew why a crown should be cushioned or a cushion crowned, and it was such a big name for the shanty, that it was diminished to 'The Crown.' But it had those four windows with crimson blinds, and the landlady was said to be a Gypsy and was followed wherever she went by a white-footed black cat that looked as if it was really a lady from a far country enchanted into a cat. The Gypsy was a most Christian body. She used to treat with unmistakeable kindness, whenever he called at the inn, a gentleman who was notoriously an atheist and teetotaler. When asked upbraidingly why, she said: 'He seems a nice gentleman, and as he is going to a place where there won't be many comforts, I think we ought to do our best to make this world as happy as possible for him.'

"Opposite to the inn was a carpenter's shop, full of windows, and I remember seeing the carpenter once at midnight there, working at a coffin all alone in the glare in the middle of the blackness. He was a mysterious man. He never touched ale. He had a soft face with silky grizzled hair and beard, large eyes, kind and yet unfriendly, and strange gentle lips as rosy as a pretty girl's. I had an extraordinary reverence for him due to his likeness to a picture at home of the greatest of the sons of carpenters. He was tall and thin, and walked like an overgrown boy. Words were rare with him. I do not think he ever spoke to me, and this silence and his ceaseless work—and especially that one midnight task—fascinated me. So I would stare for an hour at a time at him and his work, my face

73

against the window, without his ever seeming to notice me at all. He had two dogs, a majestic retriever named Ruskin who was eighteen years old, and a little black and white mongrel named Jimmy; and the two accompanied him and ignored one another. One day as I was idling along towards the shop, smelling one of those clusters of wild carrot seeds, like tiny birds' nests, which are scented like a ripe pear sweeter and juicier than ever grew on pear-tree, the carpenter came out with a gun under one arm and a spade under the other and went a short distance down the road and then into a field which belonged to him. I followed. No sooner had I begun to look over the gate than the carpenter lifted his gun and pointed it at the retriever who had his back turned and was burying a bone in a corner of the field. The carpenter fired, the old dog fell in a heap with blood running out of his mouth, and Jimmy burst out of the hedge, snatched the bone, and disappeared. If it had been anyone but the carpenter I should have thought this murder a presumptuous and cruel act; his face and its likeness taught me that it was a just act; and that, more than anything else, made justice inseparable in my mind from pain and intolerable mystery. I was overawed, and watched him from the moment when he began to dig until all that was mortal of the old dog was covered up. It seems he had been ill and a burden to himself for a long time. I thought it unjust that he should have been shot when his back was turned, and this question even drowned my indignation at the mongrel's insolence.

"I knew most of the farmers and labourers, and they were and are as distinct in my mind as the kings of England. They were local men with names so common in the churchyard that for some time I supposed it was a storehouse, rather than a resting-place, of farmers and labourers. They took small notice of me, and I was never tired of following them about the fields, ploughing, mowing, reaping, and in the milking sheds, in the orchards and the copses. Nothing is more attractive to children than a man going about his work with a kindly but complete indifference to themselves. It is a mistake to be always troubling to show interest in them, whether you feel it or not. I remember best a short, thick, dark man, with a face like a bulldog's, broader than it was long, the under-lip sticking out and up and suggesting great power and fortitude. Yet it was also a kind face, and when he was talking I could not take my eyes off it, smiling as it was kneaded up into an enormous smile, and watching the stages of the process by which it was smoothed again. When he was on his deathbed his son, who was a tailor, used to walk over every evening from the town for a gossip. The son had a wonderful skill in mimicry, and a store of tales to employ it, but at last the old man, shedding tears of laughter, had to beg him not to tell his best stories because laughing hurt so much. He died of cancer. No man could leave that neighbourhood and not be missed in a hundred ways; I missed chiefly this man's smile, which I could not help trying to reproduce on my own face long afterwards. But nobody could forget him, even had there been no better reasons, because after he died his house was never again occupied. A labourer cultivated the garden, but the house was left, and the vine leaves crawled in at the broken windows and spread wanly into the dark rooms. A storm tumbled the chimney through the roof. No ghost was talked of. The house was part of his mortal remains decaying more slowly than the rest. The labourer in the garden never pruned the vine or the apple-trees, or touched the flower borders. He was a wandering, three-quarter-witted fellow who came from nowhere and had no name but Tom. His devotion to the old man had been like a dog's. Friends or relatives or home of his own he had none, or could remember none. In fact, he had scarce any memory; when anything out of his past life came by chance into his head, he rushed to tell his master and would repeat it for days with pride and for fear of losing it, as he invariably did. One of these memories was a nonsensical rigmarole of a song which he tried to sing, but it was no more singing than talking, and resembled rather the whimper of a dog in its sleep; it had to do with a squire and a Welshman, whose accent and mistaken English might alone have made the performance black mystery. They tried to get his 'real' name out of him, but he knew only Tom. Asked who gave it to him, he said it was Mr Road, a former employer, a very cruel man whom he did not like telling about. They asked him if he was ever confirmed.

'No,' he said, 'they tried, but I could not confirm.' He would do anything for his master, rise at any hour of the night though he loved his bed, and go anywhere. Summer or Winter, he would not sleep in a house, but in a barn. Except his master's in the last illness, he would not enter any house. He was fond of beer in large quantities, but if he got drunk with it he was ashamed of himself, and might go off and not return for months: then one day he would emerge from the barn, shaking himself and smiling an awkward twisted smile and as bashful as a baby. What a place this modern world is for a man like that, now. I do not like to think he is still alive in it. All the people who could understand him are in the workhouse or the churchyard. The churchyard is the only place where he would be likely to stay long. No prison, asylum, or workhouse, could have kept him alive for many days.

"The church was like a barn except that it was nearly always empty, and only mice ever played in it. Though I went to it every Sunday I never really got over my dislike of the parson, which began in terror. He was the only man in the country who invariably wore black from top to toe. One hot, shining day I was playing in a barn, and the doors were open, so that I saw a field of poppies making the earth look as if it had caught fire in the sun; the swallows were coming in and out, and I was alone, when suddenly a black man stood in the sunny doorway. The swallows dashed and screamed at him angrily, and I thought that they would destroy themselves, for they returned again and again to within an inch of him. I could not move. He stood still, then with a smile and a cough he went away without having said a word. The next time I saw him was in the churchyard, when I was about five, and had not yet begun to attend the Church; in fact I had never entered it to my knowledge. The nurse-girl wheeled me up to the churchyard wall and stopped at the moment when the black man appeared out of the church. Behind him several men were carrying a long box between them on their shoulders, and they also were in complete black, and after them walked men, women, and children, in black; one of the older women was clinging convulsively to a stiff young man. When they had all stopped, the parson coughed and muttered something, which was followed by a rustling and silence; the woman clinging to the young man sobbed aloud, and her hair fell all over her cheeks like rain. The nurse-girl had been chatting with a few passers-by who were watching outside the wall, but as I saw the woman's hair fall I began to cry and I was hurried away. Through the lych-gate I saw a hole in the ground and everyone looking down into it as if they had lost something. At this I stopped crying and asked the girl what they were looking for; but she only boxed my ears and I cried again. When at last she told me that there was a man 'dead' in the box, and that they had put him into the ground, I felt sure that the black man was in some way the cause of the trouble. I remembered the look he had given me at the barn door, and the cough. I was filled with wonder that no one had attempted to rescue the 'dead,' and then with fear and awe at the power of the black man. Whenever I saw him in the lane I ran away, he was so very black. Nor was the white surplice ever more than a subterfuge to make him like the boys in the choir, while his unnatural voice, praying or preaching, sounded as if it came up out of the hole in the ground where the 'dead' had been put away.

"How glad I was always, to be back home from the church; though dinner was ready I walked round the garden, touching the fruit-trees one by one, stopping a minute in a corner where I could be unseen and yet look at the house and the thick smoke pouring out of the kitchen chimney. Then I rushed in and kissed my mother. The rest of the day was very still, no horses or carts going by, no sound of hoes, only the cows passing to the milkers. My father and my mother were both very silent on that day, and I felt alone and never wanted to stray far; if it was fine I kept to the garden and orchard; if wet, to the barn. The day seems in my memory to have always been either sunny or else raining with roars of wind in the woods on the hills; and I can hear the sound, as if it had been inaudible on other days, of wind and rain in the garden trees. If I climbed up into the old cherry-tree that forked close to the ground I could be entirely hidden, and I used to fancy myself alone in the world, and kept very still and silent lest I should be found out. But I gave up climbing the tree after the day when I found Mrs Partridge there before me. I never made out why she was up there, so quiet.

"Mrs Partridge was a labourer's wife who came in two or three days a week to do the rough work. I did not like her because she was always bustling about with a great noise and stir, and she did not like me because I was a spoilt, quiet child. She was deferential to all of us, and called me 'Sir'; but if I dared to touch the peel when she was baking, or the bees-wax that she rubbed her irons on when she was ironing, she talked as if she were queen or I were naught. While she worked she sang in a coarse, high-pitched voice or tried to carry on a conversation with my mother, though she might be up in the orchard. She was a little woman with a brown face and alarming glittering eyes. She was thickly covered with clothes, and when her skirts were hoisted up to her knees, as they usually were, she resembled a partridge. She was as quick and plump as a partridge. She ran instead of walking, her head forward, her hands full of clothes and clothes-pegs, and her voice resounding. No boy scrambled over gates or fences more nimbly. She feared nothing and nobody. She was harsh to her children, but when her one-eyed cat ate the Sunday dinner she could not bear to strike it, telling my mother, 'I've had the poor creature more than seven years.' She was full of idioms and proverbs, and talked better than any man has written since Cobbett. One of her proverbs has stayed fantastically in my mind, though I have forgotten the connection— 'As one door shuts another opens.' It impressed me with great mystery, and as she said it the house seemed very dark, and, though it was broad daylight and summer, I heard the wind howling in the roof just as it often did at night and on winter afternoons.

"Mrs Partridge had a husband of her own size, but with hollowed cheeks the colour of leather. Though a slight man he had broad shoulders and arms that hung down well away from his body, and this, with his bowed stiff legs, gave him a look of immense strength and stability: to this day it is hard to imagine that such a man could die. When I heard his horses going by on a summer morning I knew that it was six o'clock; when I saw them returning I knew that it was four. He was the carter, and he did nothing but work, except that once a week he went into the town with his wife, drank a pint of ale with her, and helped her to carry back the week's provisions. He needed nothing but work, out of doors, and in the stables, and physical rest indoors; and he was equally happy in both. He never said anything to disturb his clay pipe, though that was usually out. What he thought about I do not know, and I doubt if he did; but he could always break off to address his horses by name, every minute or two, in mild rebuke or cheerful congratulation, as much for his own benefit as for theirs, to remind himself that he had their company. He had full responsibility for four cart-horses, a plough, a waggon, and a dung-cart. He cared for the animals as if they had been his own: if they were restless at night he also lost his sleep. Although so busy he was never in haste, and he had time for everything save discontent. His wife did all the talking, and he had his way without taking the pipe out of his mouth. She also had her own way, in all matters but one. She was fond of dancing; he was not, and did not like to see her dance. When she did so on one tempting occasion, and confessed it, he slept the night in the barn and she did not dance again. There was a wonderful sympathy between them, and I remember hearing that when she knew that she was going to have a baby, it was he and not she that was indisposed.

"Our house was a square one of stone and tiles, having a porch and a room over it, and all covered up in ivy, convolvulus, honeysuckle, and roses, that mounted in a cloud far over the roof and projected in masses, threatening some day to pull down all with their weight, but never trimmed. The cherry-tree stretched out a long horizontal branch to the eaves at one side. In front stood two pear-trees, on a piece of lawn which was as neat as the porch was wild, and around their roots clustered a thicket of lilac and syringa, hiding the vegetable-garden beyond. These trees darkened and cooled the house, but that did not matter. In no other house did winter fires ever burn so brightly or voices sound so sweet; and outside, the sun was more brilliant than anywhere else, and the vegetable-garden was always bordered by crimson or yellow flowers. The road went close by, but it was a hollow lane,

and the heads of the passers-by did not reach up to the bottom of
our hedge, whose roots hung down before caves that were continually being deepened by frost. This hedge, thickened by
traveller's joy, bramble, and ivy, entirely surrounded us; and as it
was high as well as thick you could not look out of it except at the
sky and the hills—the road, the neighbouring fields, and all houses
being invisible. The gate, which was reached by a flight of steps up
from the road, was half-barricaded and all but hidden by brambles
and traveller's joy, and the unkempt yew-tree saluted and
drenched the stranger—in one branch a golden-crested wren
had a nest year after year.

"Two trees reigned at the bottom of the garden—at one side an
apple; at the other, just above the road, a cypress twice as high as
the house, ending in a loose plume like a black cock's tail. The
apple-tree was old, and wore as much green in winter as in summer,
because it was wrapped in ivy, every branch was furry with lichen
and moss, and the main boughs bushy with mistletoe. Each
autumn a dozen little red apples hung on one of its branches like a
line of poetry in a foreign language, quoted in a book. The thrush
used to sing there first in winter, and usually sang his last evening
song there, if it was a fine evening. Yet the cypress was my
favourite. I thought there was something about it sinister to all but
myself. I liked the smell of it, and when at last I went to the sea its
bitterness reminded me of the cypress. Birds were continually
going in and out of it, but never built in it. Only one bird sang in it,
and that was a small, sad bird which I do not know the name of. It
sang there every month of the year, it might be early or it might be
late, on the topmost point of the plume. It never sang for long, but
frequently, and always suddenly. It was black against the sky, and I
saw it nowhere else. The song was monotonous and dispirited, so
that I fancied it wanted us to go, because it did not like the cheerful
garden, and my father's loud laugh, and my mother's tripping step:
I fancied it was up there watching the clouds and very distant
things in hope of a change; but nothing came, and it sang again,
and waited, ever in vain. I laughed at it, and was not at all sorry to
see it there, for it had stood on that perch in all the happy days

80

before, and so long as it remained the days would be happy. My father did not like the bird, but he was often looking at it, and noted its absence as I did. The day after my sister died he threw a stone at it—the one time I saw him angry—and killed it. But a week later came another, and when he heard it he burst into tears, and after that he never spoke of it but just looked up to see if it was there when he went in or out of the porch. We had taller trees in the neighbourhood, such as the wych-elms and the poplars by the brook, but this was a solitary stranger and could be seen several miles away like a black pillar, as the old cherry could in blossom-time, like a white dome. You were seldom out of sight of it. It was a station for any bird flying to or from the hills. A starling stopped a minute, piped and flew off. The kestrel was not afraid to alight and look around. The nightjar used it. At twilight it was encircled by midges, and the bats attended them for half an hour. Even by day it had the sinister look which was not sinister to me: some of the night played truant and hid in it throughout the sunshine. Often I could see nothing, when I looked out of my window, but the tree and the stars that set round it, or the mist from the hills. What with this tree, and the fruit-trees, and the maples in the hedge, and the embowering of the house, I think the birds sometimes forgot the house. In the mornings, in bed, I saw every colour on the woodpigeon, and the ring on his neck, as he flew close by without swerving. At breakfast my father would say, 'There's a kestrel.' We looked up and saw nothing, but on going to the window, there was the bird hovering almost above us. I suppose its shadow or its blackening of the sky made him aware of it before he actually saw it.

"Next to us—on still days we heard the soft bell rung in the yard there at noon—was the manor-house, large, but unnoticeable among its trees. I knew nothing about the inside of it, but I went all over the grounds, filled my pockets with chestnuts, got a peach now and then from the gardener, picked up a peacock's feather. Wonderfully beautiful ladies went in and out of that old house with the squire. A century back he would have been a pillar of the commonwealth: he was pure rustic English, and his white hair and beard had an honourable look as if it had been granted to him for some rare service; no such beards are to be found now in country-houses. I do not know what he did: I doubt if there is anything for such a man to do to-day except sit for his portrait to an astonished modern painter. I think he knew men as well as horses; at least he knew everyone in that country, had known them all when he and they were boys. He was a man as English, as true to the soil, as a Ribston pippin.

"The woods on the hills were his, or at least such rights as anybody had in them were his. As for me, I got on very well in them with no right at all. Now, home and the garden were so well known, so safe, and so filled with us, that they seemed parts of us, and I only crept a little deeper into the core when I went to bed at night, like a worm in a big sweet apple. But the woods on the hills were utterly different, and within them you could forget that there was anything in the world but trees and yourself, as insignificant self, so wide and solitary were they. The trees were mostly beeches and yews, massed closely together. Nothing could grow under them. Except for certain natural sunny terraces not easily found, they covered the whole hills from top to bottom, even in the steepest parts where you could slide, run, and jump the whole distance down—about half a mile—in two minutes. The soil was dead branches and dead leaves of beech and yew. Many of the trees were dead: the stumps stood upright until they were so rotten that I could overturn them with a touch. Others hung slanting among the boughs of their companions, or were upheld by huge cables of honeysuckle or traveller's joy which had once climbed up them and flowered over their crests. Many had mysterious caverns at their roots, and as it were attic windows high up where the owls nested. The earth was a honeycomb of rabbits' burrows and foxes' earths among the bony roots of the trees, some of them stuffed with a century of dead leaves.

"Where the slope was least precipitous or had a natural ledge, two or three tracks for timber-carriages had once been made. But these had not been kept up, and were not infallible even as footpaths. They were, however, most useful guides to the terraces, where the sun shone and I could see the cypress and my mother among the sunflowers, and the far-away hills.

"On my ninth birthday they gave me an old horn that had been a huntsman's, and when I was bold and the sun was bright, I sometimes blew it in the woods, trembling while the echoes roamed among the gulfs which were hollowed in the hillsides, and my mother came out into the little garden far off. During the autumn and winter the huntsman blew his horn in the woods often for a whole day together. The root caves and old earths gave the fox more than a chance. The horses were useless. The hounds had to swim rather than run in perpetual dead leaves. If I saw the fox I tried hard not to shout and betray him, but the temptation was very strong to make the echo, for I was proud of my halloo, and I liked to see the scarlet coats, the lordly riders and the pretty ladies, and to hear the questing hound and horn, and the whips calling Ajax, Bravery, Bannister, Fury Nell, and the rest. Then at last I was glad to see the pack go by at the day's end, with sleepy heads, taking no notice of me and waving tails that looked clever as if they had eyes and ears in them, and to hear the clatter of horses dying round the end of the crescent into the outer world.

"Nobody took heed of the woods except the hunters. The timber was felled if at all by the west wind. The last keeper had long ago left his thatched cottage under the hill, where the sun shone so hot at midday on the reed-thatched shed and the green mummy of a stoat hanging on the wall. So I met nobody in the woods. I took an axe there day after day for a week and chopped a tree half through, unmolested except by the silence, which, however, wore me out with its protest.

"The woods ended at the top in a tangle of thorns, and it was there I saw my first fox. I was crawling among some brambles, amusing myself with biting off the blackberries, when a fox jumped up out of a tuft and faced me, his eyes on the level with mine. I was pleased as well as startled, never took my eyes off him, and presently began to crawl forward again. But at this the fox flashed his teeth at me with a snap, and was off before I could think of anything to say. High above these thorns stood four Scotch firs, forming a sort of gateway by which I usually re-entered the woods. Gazing up their tall stems that moved slowly and softly like a grasshopper's horns, as if they were breathing, I took my last look at the sky before plunging under beech and yew. There were always squirrels in one of them, chasing one another clattering up and down the bark, or chattering at me, close at hand, as if their nerves were shattered with surprise and indignation. When they had gone out of sight I began to run—faster and faster, running and sliding down with a force that carried me over the meadow at the foot, and across the road to the steps and home. I had ten years in that home and in those woods. Then my father died: I went to school: I entered an office. Those ten years were reality. Everything since has been scarcely more real than the world was when it was still cut off by the hills across the valley, and I looked lazily towards it from under the cypress where the little bird sang. There is nothing to rest on, nothing to make a man last like the old men I used to see in cottage gardens or at gateways in the valley of the Uther."

"Well," said Mr Morgan once, "I don't often agree with Mr Torrance, but I am very glad he exists."

CHAPTER XI

To Mr Stodham, I think, Mr Torrance's books were the man. He—perhaps he alone in England—possessed a full set of the thirty-three volumes produced by Mr Torrance under his own name in thirteen years. "It is wonderful," said Ann once, "that the dancing of a pen over a sheet of paper can pay the rent and the baker's bill, and it hardly seems right. But, still, it appears there are people born that can do nothing else, and they must live like the rest of us. . . . And I will say that Mr Torrance is one of the best of us, though he has that peculiarity."

Mr Stodham could not trust himself to speak. He really liked Ann: furthermore, he knew that she was wiser than he: finally, everyone at that moment had something better to think of, because Jack and Roland had put on the gloves. Mr Stodham, consequently, quoted George Borrow:

"There's the wind on the heath, brother; if I could only feel that, I would gladly live for ever. Dosta, we'll now go to the tents and put on the gloves; and I'll try to make you feel what a sweet thing it is to be alive, brother."

Jack overheard him, and at the end of the round said, "What was that, Mr Stodham? say it again." When the words of Jasper had been repeated, "Jolly good," said Jack, "but what puzzles me is how a man who knew that could bother to write a book. There must have been something the matter with him. Perhaps he didn't really believe what he wrote." And so they had another round.

Mr Stodham liked everything at Abercorran House. Liking was his chief faculty and there it had unstinted exercise. Probably he liked the very wife whom he escaped by going either to the country or to Abercorran House. An accident had first brought him among the Morgans. One day as he happened to be passing down the farm

85

lane a child threw a ball unintentionally over into the Wilderness. After it went Mr Stodham in an instant, not quite missing the nails at the top of the fence. The long grass of the Wilderness and his own bad sight kept the ball hidden until the child went away in despair, unknown to him, for he continued the search. There perhaps he would have been searching still, if the Wilderness had not been built over, and if Roland had not come along and found man and ball almost in the same moment. Here the matter could not end. For Mr Stodham, unawares, had been reduced by a nail in the fence to a condition which the public does not tolerate. It seems that he offered to wait for nightfall when Roland had pointed out his misfortune. He was stubborn, to the verge of being abject, in apologising for his presence, and, by implication, for his existence, and in not wishing to cause any trouble to Roland or the family. Gently but firmly Roland lured him upstairs and gave him a pair of trousers beyond reproach. On the following day when he reappeared, bearing the trousers and renewed apologies, the family, out in the yard, was in full parliament assembled. He made a little speech, cheered by everyone but Higgs. Presumably he was so fascinated by the scene that the cheering did not disconcert him. He could not get away, especially as his stick had been seized by Spot the fox-terrier, who was now with apparently no inconvenience to himself, being whirled round and round on the end of it by Jack. Ann came out with his own trousers thoroughly reformed, and she had to be thanked. Lastly, Mr Morgan carried him off before the stick had been recovered. Next day, therefore, he had to come again in search of the stick, a priceless favourite before Spot had eaten it. Mr Morgan consoled him and cemented the acquaintance by giving him an ash stick with a handle formed by Nature in the likeness of a camel's head. Mr Morgan said that the stick had been cut on Craig-y-Dinas—the very place where the ash stick was cut, which a certain Welshman was carrying on London Bridge when he was espied by a magician, who asked to be taken to the mother tree, which in as long as it takes to walk three hundred miles was done, with the result that a cave was found on Craig-y-Dinas, full of treasure which was guarded by King Arthur and his knights, who were, however, sleeping a sleep only to be disturbed by a certain bell, which the Welshman by ill luck did ring, with the predicted result, that the king and his knights rose up in their armour and so terrified him that he forgot the word which would have sent them to sleep again, and he dropped all his treasure, ran for his life, and could never more find cave, stick, or magician for all his seeking. Mr Stodham responded in a sententious pretty speech, saying in effect that with such a stick he needed no other kind of treasure than those it would inevitably conduct him to—the hills, rivers, woods, and meadows of the home-counties, and some day, he hoped, to Craig-y-Dinas itself.

Thus Mr Stodham came again and again, to love, honour, and obey the ways of Abercorran House, just as he did the entirely different ways of Mrs Stodham's house. He, and no other, taught Philip the way to that piece of country which became ours. Harry and Lewis, still under ten, awakened in him a faculty for spinning yarns. What they were nobody but those three knew; for the performance was so special and select that the two boys formed the sole audience. They revealed nothing of what enchanted them. Or was there anything more than at first appeared in Harry's musing remark on being questioned about Mr Stodham's stories: "Mr Stodham's face is like a rat," a remark which was accompanied by a nibbling grimace which caused smiles of recognition and some laughter? "Yes," added Lewis, penitent at the laughter he had provoked, "a *very good* rat!" Perhaps the shy, sandy man's shrunken face was worked up to an unwonted—and therefore comical—freedom of expression in the excitement of these tales, and this fascinated the boys and made them his firm supporters. He was a tall, thin, sandy-haired, sandy-bearded man with spectacles. As if tobacco smoke had mummified him, his face was of a dried yellow. He stooped slightly and walked rapidly with long strides. Nobody had professed to find anything great or good in him, yet several different kinds of men spoke of him with liking as well as pity. If there was something exceptional about this most ordinary man, it was his youthfulness. It had been said that he was too dull to grow old. But youthful he was, though it is hard to say how, since he

truly was dull, and if he had not been indolent must have been a
bore—but he was too modest for anyone to allow him to bore. As
you walked behind him you had little doubt of his youthfulness.
Something in the loose-jointed lightness and irresponsibility of his
gait suggested a boy, and if you had been following him with this
thought, and he turned round to greet you, the wrinkled, smoky
face was a great surprise. There was something in his nature
corresponding to this loose-jointed walk. The dogs, I think, knew
it: they could do what they liked with him, and for them he carried
sugar as a regular cargo.

Thus, Mr Stodham began to be interwoven with that fellow-
ship. I was perhaps too old for his romantic tales, but I have heard
him telling Mr Morgan what he considered interesting in his own
life. Whatever it was, it revealed his shyness, or his excitability, or
his innocence. Once he gave a long explanation of how he came to
set an uncommon value on a certain book which he was lending to
Mr Morgan. Some winters before, something caused him to wake
at midnight and sit up to listen, in spite of the usual powerful
inclination to sleep again. At a sharp noise on the pane he threw
up the window. All the flints of the road were clear in an unusual
light. The white face of a policeman was looking up at him, and he
heard the words "Fire! . . . Come down." Rapidly half dressing as if
executing an order which he did not understand, he was outside on
the pavement in a minute. It was next door. The building was
losing all resemblance to a barber's shop; like mad birds the flames
flew across it and out at the shuttered windows. The policeman was
hammering at the door, to waken those who were in their beds
above the fire. Heavily they slept, and some minutes passed before
a man came down carrying an umbrella, a woman arranging her
hair. The shriek of a cat followed them out of the door, but so also
did the flames. Soon the shop was an oblong box containing one
great upright body of fire, through which could be seen the twisted
skeleton remains of iron bedsteads. Quietly the street had become
packed with onlookers—curious neighbours, passers-by, and a few
night-wanderers who had souls above merely keeping warm by
standing against the walls of bakeries. There were three fire

engines. With a low hum the jets of water yielded themselves to the fire and were part of it. Suddenly a fireman noticed that Mr Stodham's own window was lit from within, thought that the flames had penetrated so far, and was about to direct the hose on it when Mr Stodham shook off the charm of the tumultuous glare to explain that he had left a lamp burning. The man went with him into the house, but could find no fire. Left alone in his room Mr Stodham noticed that it was hot, pleasantly hot for a January midnight. The wall that he leaned against was pleasant until he remembered the fire on the other side. He made haste to save his papers. Instead of sorting them roughly there, he proposed to remove, not the separate drawers, but the whole desk. He forgot that it had only entered the house, in the first place, after having the castors detached, and omitting to do this now, he wedged it firmly between the walls and so barricaded the main passage of the house. He took out all the contents of all the drawers, deposited them with a neighbour whom he had never before seen. Then he returned to his room. He was alone with his books, and had to choose among them, which he should take and save. They numbered several hundred, including a shelf of the very first books he had read to himself. A large proportion consisted of the books of his youth. Having been lived through by the eager, docile Stodham, these poems, romances, essays, autobiographies, had each a genuine personality, however slight the difference of its cover from its neighbour's. Another class represented aspirations, regrets, oblivions: half cut, dustier than the rest, these wore strange, sullen, ironical, or actually hostile looks. Some had been bought because it was inevitable that a young man should have a copy. Others, chiefly volumes in quarto or folio, played something like the parts of family portraits in a house of one of the new-rich. An unsuspecting ostentation had gone with some affection to their purchase. They gave a hint of "the dark backward and abysm of time" to that small room, dingy, but new. . . . He leaned against the hot wall, receiving their various looks, returning them. Several times he bent forward to clutch this one or that, but saw another which he could not forsake for it, and so left both. He moved up

close to the rows: he stood on tip-toe, he knelt. Some books he
touched, others he opened. He put each one back. The room was
silent with memory. He might have put them all in safety by this
time. The most unexpected claims were made. For example, there
was a black-letter "Morte d'Arthur" in olive calf. He had paid so
much for it that he had to keep its existence secret: brown paper
both concealed and protected it. He did, in fact, put this with a few
others, chosen from time to time, on a chair. Only a very few were
without any claims—histories and the like, of which there are
thousands of copies, all the same. The unread and never-to-be-
read volumes put in claims unexpectedly. No refusal could be made
without a qualm. He looked at the select pile on the chair
dissatisfied. Rather than take them only he would go away empty.
"You had better look sharp, sir," said a fireman, vaulting over the
desk. Mr Stodham looked at the mute multitude of books and saw
all in a flash. Nevertheless not one could he make up his mind to
rescue. But on the mantelpiece lay a single book until now
unnoticed—a small eighteenth century book in worn contemporary binding, an illustrated book of travels in Africa by a French-
man—which he had long ago paid twopence for and discontinued
his relations with it. He swiftly picked up this book and was,
therefore, able to lend it to Mr Morgan for the sake of the plates.
But after all he saved all his other books also. The fire did not reach
his house, and the one thing damaged was the desk which the
firemen had to leap on to and over in passing through to the back of
the house.

Mr Stodham, in spite of professing a poor opinion of the subject,
was delighted in his quiet way to speak of himself. He was at this
time a nearly middle-aged clerk, disappointed in a tranquil style,
and beginning to regard it as something to his credit that when he
had been four years married he had talked a good deal of going to
the colonies. If only he had gone—his imagination was unequal to
the task of seeing what might have happened if only he had gone.
The regret of pretence of it gave him a sort of shadowy grandeur by
suggesting that it was from a great height he had fallen to his
present position in a suburban maisonette. Here by some means he

had secured to himself the exclusive rights to a little room known as "The Study." This room was narrower than it was high, and allowed no more than space for his table between the two walls of books, when he sat facing the French window, with the door behind. He looked out on a pink almond-tree, and while this flowered he could see nothing else but the tree and the south-east sky above it; at other seasons the hind parts of many houses like his own were unmistakeable. At night a green blind was let down over the window before the lamp was lit. In this room, and in no other place but Abercorran House, he was at home. Seated at that table, smoking, he felt equal to anything with which his wife or the world could afflict him. He desired no change in the room, beyond a slowly increasing length to accommodate his increasing books. He would have liked to open the windows more often than, being of the French pattern, was deemed safe. The room was completely and unquestionably his own. For his wife it was too shabby and too much out of her influence; she would not take her fingers from the door-handle when she had to enter it. His children were stiff and awed in it, because in earlier days he had been strict in demanding silence in its neighbourhood. Much as he wished that they would forget the old rule they could not; he liked to see them standing at the door looking towards him and the window, but they made haste to be off. As to the servant, she dreaded being caught in the room since the mistress had commanded her to dust it daily, and the master to leave it to him.

Mr Morgan, Mr Torrance, and in later years myself, he admitted to the Study. Acquaintances he received with his wife in their clean and expensive drawing-room. Husband and wife were in harmony when entertaining a few of those whom Mrs Stodham called their friends. On these rare occasions the defensive combination of her slightly defiant pride and his kindly resignation was a model of unconscious tact. If there was a man—which seldom came about—Mr Stodham would ask him into the Study. The gas was slowly lighted, the gas-stove more slowly or not at all. The intruder would remark what a lot of books there were, and how he never had any time for reading. There was only one chair, and he was compelled to sit in it and to light a cigarette. Mr Stodham himself was loth to smoke there in profane company, but dallied with an unaccustomed cigarette, or, if he took a pipe, soon rapped out on the stove with it some variation upon the theme of discontent. In either case his gentle but disturbed presence hung oppressively on the visitor, who very soon took the hint from that helpless but determined face, to propose a return to the drawing-room. There Mrs Stodham frequently made the remark: "What a lot of books John has," nodding complacently and with the implication partly that she despised them, partly that she saw their worth as a family distinction. At the end of such an evening or after any unpleasantness Mr Stodham would go into the Study, stick an unlit pipe between his teeth, open a book and read very slowly, stretching his legs out, for five minutes, then sigh, stand up and look along the rows of books without seeing them, and go up to bed before he had defined his dissatisfaction.

The Study was the scene of the most extraordinary thing he had to relate. Once when he had been lying for several days in bed, weak and fevered, he had a strong desire to go downstairs to the Study. Darkness and tea-time were near, his wife and children were out, doubtless the servant was reading something by the light of the red-hot kitchen grate. The house was silent. Slowly the invalid went down and laid his fingers on the handle of his door, which was opposite the foot of the stairs. An unusual feeling of quiet expectancy had stolen on him; nothing, he said, could have astonished him at that moment. He had, however, no idea of what he was expecting until he had opened the door to its full extent. Thus was disclosed, between his table and the window, a beautiful female figure, half sitting, half reclining, as if asleep, among a number of books which had remained on the floor during his illness. Though he had not put on his spectacles before coming down he saw perfectly, so clearly, as he said, that she seemed to gleam, as if it was still full day with her. Her beautiful long black hair was confined by a narrow fillet of gold, which made clear the loveliness of her head. He said that only Mr Torrance could describe her properly. No, he affirmed, if people smiled, it did not occur to him that the nude looked awkward near a gas-stove. Nor had she any more need of its warmth than the Elgin Marbles or the Bacchus in Titian's "Bacchus and Ariadne." Yet she was not of marble or paint, but of flesh, though he had seen nothing of the kind in his life. Her shoulders moved with her breathing, and this as well as her attitude proclaimed that she was mourning, some seconds before he heard her sob. He thought that the figure and posture were the same as those in a Greek statue which he had seen long before, in London or Paris. They had the remoteness and austerity of marble along with something delicate, transient, and alive. But if there could have been a doubt whether she was flesh or stone, there was none that she was divine. In what way she was divine he could not tell, but certainly she was, though in no visible way was she different from the women of pictures and statues. He did not feel that she would notice him. He was not shocked, or curious, but calm and still expectant. He drew a deep breath and tried to make his trembling body stand quite still by leaning against the wall to watch. He did not suppose that she had come into his room in the ordinary way. He had, on the other hand, a conviction that she had something to do with his books, that she had emerged from them or one of them. A gap in the bottom shelf, where stood the largest books, caught his eye and thrust itself forward as a cave whence she had come. Yet she was as white as Aphrodite newly risen from the unsailed ocean, and she diffused a sense of open air, of space, of the wild pure air, about her, as if she lay upon a rock at the sea edge or among mountain flowers instead of in this narrow room. He concluded in a reasonable way that she was one of the poets' nymphs whom he had so often read of with lazy credulity. Actually the words ran into his mind:

> "Arethusa arose
>   From her couch of snows
> In the Acroceraunian mountains—
>   From cloud and from crag,
>   With many a jag,
> Shepherding her bright fountains."

But he did not accept her as the Sicilian river. Other words crept through his mind, as of "lorn Urania . . . most musical of mourners," and of "lost Echo" seated "amid the voiceless mountains." Still his brain flew on, next causing him to see in her an incarnation of the morning star, for from brow to foot she was very bright. But he came back again to the idea of some goddess, or muse, or grace, or nymph, or Dryad—the word Dryad recurring several times as if by inspiration; and thereafter he referred to her as the Dryad.

It seemed to be the sound of the door-handle released some time after the door was closed that caused her suddenly to become silent and to raise her sea-gray glittering eyes towards him. She was gasping for breath. "Air," she cried, "Air—the wide air and light—air and light." Mr Stodham rushed forward past her and threw open one of the French windows. She turned towards the air, drinking it with her lips and also with her hands which opened and closed with motions like leaves under water. Mr Stodham could not open the second window. "Air," cried the Dryad. So he thrust steadily and then violently at the frame with his whole body until the window gave way, splintering and crashing. Still moving as if drowning and vainly trying to rise, the Dryad cried out for more of the air which now streamed into the Study. By stretching out her hands now up and now on either side she implored to be surrounded by an ocean of air. To Mr Stodham this was a command. Sideways with head lowered he leaned heavily against both walls in turn, struggling to overthrow them. He strode backwards and forwards along the bookshelves, striking fiercely here and there in the hope that the wall would yield and let in the heavenly air for the Dryad. When he thought this vain he ran from room to room throwing open or smashing each window until all had been done. "More air," she shouted, The last room was the drawing-room. Its windows having been smashed, he set about doing what he had run out of his study to do. In the middle of the drawing-room he began to make a fire. From floor to ceiling the eager flames leapt at a bound; a widening circle of carpet smouldered; and Mr Stodham, crouching low, shivering, holding his hands to the heat, muttered "More air," like an incantation. "The Dryad must have more air. We must all have more air. Let the clean fire burn down these walls and all the walls of London. So there will be more air, and she will be free, all will be free." As the carpet began to smoulder under him he hopped from one foot to another, not muttering now, but shrieking, "More air," and at last leaping high as the flames, he ran straight out into the street. He ran as if he were trying to escape himself—which he was; for his nightgown and dressing-gown flared out in sparks behind him, and from these he was running. He twisted and leapt in his race, as if he had a hope of twisting or leaping out of the flames. . . .

This scene was regarded by us as humorous—I suppose because we knew that Mr Stodham had survived it—but by Ann as terrible. She had a great kindness for Mr Stodham; she even proposed to deliver him from his wife by providing him with a room at Abercorran House: but if he was not content with his servitude he could not imagine another state. . .

Probably he fell down unconscious from his burns and exhaustion: he remembered no more when many days later the delirium left him. That he had attempted to set his house on fire was noted as an extraordinary frenzy of influenza: Mrs Stodham, suspecting a malicious motive for starting the fire in her drawing-room, particularly resented it. Such portions of the story as he betrayed in his delirium drove her to accuse him of having a shameful and disgusting mind.

On coming down to the Study from the sick room again he saw no Dryad. He opened wide the new French windows, and stood looking at the dark bole of the almond-tree, slender and straight, and all its blossom suspended in one feathery pile against the sky. The airy marble of the white clouds, the incorporeal sweetness of the flowers, the space and majesty of the blue sky, the freshness of the air, each in turn and all together recalled the Dryad. He shed tears in an intense emotion which was neither pleasure nor pain.

Aurelius had a great admiration for Mr Stodham on the ground that he did not write a poem about the Dryad. The story appealed also to Ann. She referred in awe to "Mr Stodham's statue." She said: "There was a statue in that condition in the church at home. Some renowned artist carved it for a memorial to the Earl's only daughter. But I could not abide it in the cold, dark, old place. It wanted to be out under the ash-trees, or in among the red roses and ferns. I did think it would have looked best of all by the waterfall. These statues are a sort of angels, and they don't seem natural under a roof with ordinary people. Out of doors it is different, or it would be, though I haven't seen angels or statues out of doors. But I have seen bathers, and they look as natural as birds."

"You are right, Ann," said Mr Morgan, "and prettier than birds. The other Sunday when I was out walking early I found a path that took me for some way alongside a stream. There was a Gypsy caravan close to the path, three or four horses scattered about, an old woman at the fire, and several of the party in the water. I hurried on because I saw that the swimmers were girls. But there was no need to hurry. Two of them, girls of about fifteen with coal-black hair, caught sight of me, and climbed out on to the bank before my eyes to beg. I walked on quickly to give them a chance of reconsidering the matter, but it was no use. Sixpence was the only thing that would turn them back. I wish now I had not been so hasty in giving it. The girl put it in her mouth, after the usual blessing, and ran back with her companion to the water. They wanted money as well as air, Stodham. Your visitor was less alive."

"For shame, sir," interjected Ann, "she was not a Gypsy. She was an honourable statue, and there is no laugh in the case at all."

"Oh, but there is, Ann, and there always will be a laugh for some one in these matters so long as some one else chooses to be as solemn as a judge in public about them, and touchy, too, Ann. Don't let us pretend or even try to be angels. We have not the figure for it. I think there is still a long future for men and women, if they have more and more air, and enough sixpences to let them bathe, for example, in peace."

"Very good," concluded Ann, "but a bit parsonified, too." She would have added something, but could no longer ignore the fact that close by stood the tall old watercress-man, Jack Horseman, patiently waiting for the right moment to touch his hat. His Indian complexion had come back to the old soldier, he was slightly tipsy, and he had a bunch of cow-slips in his hat. Mr Morgan disappeared. Ann went in with the watercress for change. Philip and I took possession of Jack, to ask if he had found that blackthorn stick he had often promised us.

CHAPTER XII

GREEN AND SCARLET

ONE evening Aurelius was telling Mr Stodham about the "battle of the green and scarlet." "It took place in your country," said he to the good man, too timid to be incredulous.

"No," answered Mr Stodham, "I never heard of it."

"You shall," said Aurelius, and told the tale.

"The first thing that I can remember is that a tall, gaunt man in green broke out of a dark forest, leaping extravagantly, super-humanly, but rhythmically, and wildly singing; and that he was leading an army to victory. As he carved and painted himself on my mind I knew without effort what had gone before this supreme moment.

"It was late afternoon in winter. No light came from the misted, invisible sky, but the turf of the bare hill-top seemed of itself to breathe up a soft illumination. Where this hill-top may be I know not, but at the time of which I am speaking I was on foot in broad daylight and on a good road in the county of Hampshire.

"The green man, the extravagant leaper and wild singer, broke out of the hillside forest at the head of a green army. His leaping and his dancing were so magnificent that his followers might at first have been mistaken for idle spectators. The enemy came, clad in scarlet, out of the forest at the opposite side of the hilltop. The two were advancing to meet upon a level plateau of smooth, almost olive turf. . . .

"For days and nights the steep hillside forest had covered the manœuvres of the forces. Except one or two on each side they had seen and heard nothing of one another, so dark were the trees, the mists so dense and of such confusing motion; and that those few had seen or heard their enemies could only be guessed, for they were found dead. Day and night the warriors saw pale mist, dark trees, darker earth, and the pale faces of their companions, alive or dead. What they heard was chiefly the panting of breathless men on the steeps, but sometimes also the drip of the sombre crystal mist-beads, the drenched flight of great birds and their shrieks of alarm or of resentment at the invaders, the chickadeedee of little birds flitting about them without fear, the singing of thrushes in thorns at the edges of the glades.

"In the eventless silence of the unknown forest each army, and the scarlet men more than the green, had begun to long for the conflict, if only because it might prove that they were not lost, forgotten, marooned, in the heart of the mist, cut off from time and from all humanity save the ancient dead whose bones lay in the barrows under the beeches. Therefore it was with joy that they heard the tread of their enemies approaching across the plain. When they could see one another it was to the scarlet men as if they had sighted home; to the green men it was as if a mistress was beckoning. They forgot the endless strange hills, the dark trees, the curst wizard mist. It no longer seemed to them that the sheep-bells, bubbling somewhere out of sight, came from flocks who were in that world which they had unwillingly and unwittingly left for ever.

"The scarlet men were very silent; if there were songs in the heads of two or three, none sang. They looked neither to left nor to right; they saw not their fellows, but only the enemy. The breadth of the plain was very great to them. With all their solidity they could hardly endure the barren interval—it had been planned that they should wait for the charge, but it was felt now that such a pause might be too much for them. Ponderous and stiff, not in a straight line, nor in a curve, nor with quite natural irregularity, but in half a dozen straight lines that never made one, they came on, like rocks moving out against the tide. I noticed that they were modern red-coats armed with rifles, their bayonets fixed.

"The green men made a curved irregular front like the incoming sea. They rejoiced separately and together in these minutes of approach. And they sang. Their song was one which the enemy took to be mournful because it had in it the spirit of the mountain mists as well as of the mountains. It saddened the hearts of the enemy mysteriously; the green men themselves it filled, as a cup with wine, with the certainty of immortality. They turned their eyes frequently towards their nearest companions, or they held their heads high, so that their gaze did not take in the earth or anything upon it. The enemy they scarcely saw. They saw chiefly their leaping leader and his mighty twelve.

"The first love of the scarlet men for the enemy had either died, or had turned into hate, fear, indignation, or contempt. There may have been joy among them, but all the passions of the individuals were blended into one passion—if such it could be called—of the mass, part contempt for the others, part confidence in themselves. But among the green men first love had grown swiftly to a wild passion of joy.

"The broad scarlet men pushed forward steadily.

"The tall green hero danced singing towards them. His men leaped after him—first a company of twelve, who might have been his brethren; then the whole green host, lightly and extravagantly. The leader towered like a fountain of living flame. Had he stood still he must have been gaunt and straight like a beech-tree that stands alone on the crest of a sea-beholding hill. He was neither young nor old—or was he both young and old like the gods? In his blue eyes burnt a holy and joyous fire. He bore no weapon save a dagger in his right hand, so small that to the enemy he appeared unarmed as he leaped towards them. First he hopped, then he leaped with one leg stretched forward and very high, and curved somewhat in front of the other, while at the same time the arm on the opposite side swung across his body. But, in fact, whenever I looked at him—and I saw chiefly him—he was high in the air, with his head uplifted and thrown back, his knee almost at the height of his chin. He also sang that seeming sorrowful melody of the mountain joy, accented to an extravagant exultation by his leaping and the flashing of his eyes.

"If he had not been there doubtless the twelve would have astonished the scarlet men and myself just as much, for they too were tall, danced the same leaping dance, sang the mountain song with the same wild and violent joy, and were likewise armed only with short daggers.

"Suddenly the leader stopped; the twelve stopped; the green army stopped; all were silent. The scarlet men continued to advance, not without glancing at one another for the first time, with inquiry in their looks, followed by scorn; they expected the enemy to turn and fly. They had no sooner formed this opinion than the tall green leader leaped forward again singing, the twelve leaped after him, the sea-like edge of the green army swayed onward. Almost a smile of satisfaction spread over the stiff faces of their opponents, for there was now but a little distance between the armies; how easily they would push through that frivolous prancing multitude—if indeed it ever dared to meet their onset. This was the one fear of the scarlet men, that the next minute was not to see the clash and the victory, that they would have to plunge once more into the forest, the mist, the silence, after a foe that seemed to them as inhuman as those things and perhaps related to them.

'Suddenly again the green leader was rigid, his song ceased. The twelve, the whole green army, were as statues. A smile grew along the line of the scarlet men when they had conquered their surprise, a smile of furious pity for such a dancing-master and his dancing-school—a smile presently of uneasiness as the seconds passed and they could hear only the sound of their own tread. The silence of all those men unnerved them. Now . . . would the green men turn? Some of the scarlet men, eager to make sure of grappling with the enemy, quickened their step, but not all. The green men did not turn. Once again the dance and the song leaped up, this time as if at a signal from the low sun which smote across the green leader's breast, like a shield, and like a banner. Wilder than ever the dance and the song of the green men. The scarlet men could see their eyes now, and even the small daggers like jewels in the hands of the leaders. Some were still full of indignant hate and already held the dancers firm on the points of their bayonets. Some thought that there was a trick, they knew not how it might end. Some wished to wait kneeling, thus to receive the dancers on their steadfast points.

Some were afraid, looking to left and right for a sign. One tripped intentionally and fell. The line became as jagged as if it were a delicate thing blown by the wind. The green leader cut the line in two without stopping his dance, leaving his dagger in the throat of a rifleman. Not one of the twelve but penetrated the breaking line in the course of the dance. The whole green army surged through the scarlet without ceasing their song, which seemed to hover above them like spray over waves. Then they turned.

"The scarlet men did not turn. They ran swiftly now, and it was their backs that met the spears of the green men as they crowded into the forest. The tall, weaponless, leaping singer seemed everywhere, above and round about, turning the charge and thrust of the green men into a lovely and a joyous thing like the arrival of Spring in March, making the very trees ghastly to the scarlet fugitives running hither and thither silently to their death. Not one of the defeated survived, for the few that eluded their pursuers could not escape the mist, nor yet the song of the green leader, except by death, which they gave to themselves in sadness.

"I cannot wonder that the hero's dancing and singing were not to be withstood by his enemies, since to me it was divine and so moving that I could not help trying to imitate both song and dance while I was walking and dreaming."

"Nothing like that ever happened to me," said Mr Stodham. "But I thought you meant a real battle. It was lucky you weren't run over if you were dreaming like that along the road."

"I suppose I was not born to be run over," said Aurelius.

CHAPTER XIII

NED OF GLAMORGAN

LONG after his celebrated introduction to Abercorran House, and soon after Philip and I had been asking old Jack again about the blackthorn stick, Mr Stodham was reminded of the story of the Welshman on London Bridge who was carrying a hazel stick cut on Craig-y-Dinas. "Do you remember it?" asked Mr Morgan.

"Certainly I do," replied Mr Stodham, "and some day the stick you gave me from that same Craig-y-Dinas shall carry me thither."

"I hope it will. It is a fine country for a man to walk in with a light heart, or, the next best thing, with a heavy heart. They will treat you well, because they will take you for a red-haired Welshman and you like pastry. But what I wanted to say was that the man who first told that story of Craig-y-Dinas was one of the prime walkers of the world. Look at this portrait of him. . . ."

Here Mr Morgan opened a small book of our grandfather's time which had for a frontispiece a full-length portrait of a short, old, spectacled man in knee breeches and buckled shoes, grasping a book in one hand, a very long staff in the other.

"Look at him. He was worthy to be immortalised in stained glass. He walked into London from Oxford one day and mentioned the fact to some acquaintances in a bookshop. They were rather hard of believing, but up spoke a stranger who had been observing the pedestrian, his way of walking, the shape of his legs, and the relative position of his knees and ankles whilst standing erect. This man declared that the Welshman could certainly have done the walk without fatigue; and he ought to have known, for he was the philosopher, Walking Stewart.

"It was as natural for this man in the picture to walk as for the sun to shine. You would like to know England, Mr Stodham, as he knew Wales, especially Glamorgan. Rightly was he entitled 'Iolo

Morganwg,' or Edward of Glamorgan, or, rather, Ned of Glamorgan. The name will outlive most stained glass, for one of the finest collections of Welsh history, genealogies, fables, tales, poetry, etc., all in old manuscripts, was made by him, and was named after him in its published form—'Iolo Manuscripts.' He was born in Glamorgan, namely at Penon, in 1746, and when he was eighty he died at Flimstone in the same county.

"As you may suppose, he was not a rich man, and nobody would trouble to call him a gentleman. But he was an Ancient Briton, and not the last one: he said once that he always possessed the freedom of his thoughts and the independence of his mind 'with an Ancient Briton's warm pride.'

"His father was a stonemason, working here, there, and everywhere, in England and Wales, in town and country. When the boy first learnt his alphabet, it was from the letters cut by his father on tombstones. His mother—the daughter of a gentleman—undoubtedly a gentleman, for he had 'wasted a pretty fortune'—taught him to read from the songs in a 'Vocal Miscellany.' She read Milton, Pope, 'The Spectator,' 'The Whole Duty of Man,' and 'Religio Medici,' and sang as well. But the boy had to begin working for his father at the age of nine. Having such a mother, he did not mix with other children, but returned nightly to read or talk with her, or, if he did not, he walked by himself in solitary places. Later on, he would always read by himself in the dinner-hour instead of going with his fellow-workmen to the inn. Once he was left, during the dinner-hour, in charge of a parsonage that was being repaired, and, having his own affairs to mind, he let all the fowls and pigs in. His father scolded him, and he went off, as the old man supposed, to pout for a week or two with his mother's people at Aberpergwm, near Pont Neath Vaughan. It was, however, some months before he reappeared—from London, not Aberpergwm. Thus, in his own opinion, he became 'very pensive, very melancholy, and very stupid,' but had fits of 'wild extravagance.' And thus, at the time of his mother's death, though he was twenty-three, he was 'as ignorant of the world as a new-born child.' Without his mother he could not stay in the house, so he set off on a long wandering. He went hither and thither over a large part of England and Wales, 'studying chiefly architecture and other sciences that his trade required.'"

"There was a mason," said Mr Stodham, "such as Ruskin wanted to set carving evangelists and kings."

"No. He knew too much, or half-knew too much. Besides, he hated kings. . . . Those travels confirmed him in the habit of walking. He was too busy and enthusiastic ever to have become an eater, and he found that walking saved him still more from eating. He could start early in the morning and walk the forty-three miles into Bristol without any food on the way; and then, after walking about the town on business, and breaking his fast with bread and butter and tea, and sleeping in a friend's chair, could walk back again with no more food; and, moreover, did so of choice, not from any beastly principle or necessity. He travelled thus with 'more alacrity and comfort,' than at other times when he had taken food more frequently. He always was indifferent to animal food and wine. Tea was his vice, tempered by sugar and plenty of milk and cream. Three or four distinct brews of an evening suited him. Once a lady assured him that she was handing him his sixteenth cup. He was not a teetotaller, though his verses for a society of journeymen masons 'that met weekly to spend a cheerful hour at the moderate and restricted expense of fourpence,' are no better than if he had been a teetotaller from his cradle:

> "'Whilst Mirth and good ale our warm spirits recruit,
> We'll drunk'ness avoid, that delight of a brute:
> Of matters of State we'll have nothing to say,
> Wise Reason shall rule and keep Discord away.
> Whilst tuning our voices Jocundity sings,
> Good fellows we toast, and know nothing of kings:
> But to those who have brightened the gloom of our lives,
> Give the song and full bumper—our sweethearts and wives.'

At one time he made a fixed resolve not to *sit* in the public room of an ale-house, because he feared the conviviality to which his talent for song-writing conduced. But it is a fact that a man who lives out of doors can eat and drink anything, everything, or almost nothing, and thrive beyond the understanding of quacks.

"Iolo walked night and day, and would see a timid gentleman home at any hour if only he could have a chair by his fireside to sleep. He got to prefer sleeping in a chair partly because his asthma forbade him to lie down, partly because it was so convenient to be able to read and write up to the last moment and during any wakeful hours. With a table, and pen, ink, paper, and books beside him, he read, wrote, and slept, at intervals, and at dawn usually let himself out of the house for a walk. During a visit to the Bishop of St David's at Abergwili he was to be seen in the small hours pacing the hall of the episcopal palace, in his nightcap, a book in one hand, a candle in the other. Probably he read enormously, but too much alone, and with too little intercourse with other readers. Besides his native Welsh he taught himself English, French, Latin and Greek. His memory was wonderful, but he had no power of arrangement; when he came to write he could not find his papers without formidable searches, and when found could not put them in an available form. I imagine he did not treat what he read, like most of us, as if it were removed several degrees from what we choose to call reality. Everything that interested him at all he accepted eagerly unless it was one of the few things he was able to condemn outright as a lie. I suppose it was the example of Nebuchadnezzar that made him try one day 'in a thinly populated part of North Wales' eating nothing but grass, until the very end, when he gave way to bread and cheese.

"He had a passion for antiquities."

"What an extraordinary thing," ejaculated Mr Stodham.

"Not very," said Mr Morgan. "He was acquisitive and had little curiosity. He was a collector of every sort and quality of old manuscript. Being an imperfectly self-educated man he probably got an innocent conceit from his learned occupation . . ."

"But how could he be an old curiosity man, and such an out-door man as well?"

"His asthma and pulmonary trouble, whatever it was, probably drove him out of doors. Borrow, who was a similar man of a

106

different class, was driven out in the same way as a lad. Iolo's passion for poetry was not destroyed, but heightened, by his travels. God knows what poetry meant to him. But when he was in London, thinking of Wales and the white cots of Glamorgan, he wrote several stanzas of English verse. Sometimes he wrote about nymphs and swains, called Celia, Damon, Colin, and the like. He wrote a poem to Laudanum:

> " 'O still exert thy soothing power,
> Till Fate leads on the welcom'd hour,
>   To bear me hence away;
> To where pursues no ruthless foe,
> No feeling keen awakens woe,
>   No faithless friends betray.' "

"I could do no worse than that," murmured Mr Stodham confidently.

"He wrote a sonnet to a haycock, and another to Hope on an intention of emigrating to America:

> " 'Th' American wilds, where Simplicity's reign
> Will cherish the Muse and her pupil defend . . .
> I'll dwell with Content in the desert alone.'

They were blessed days when Content still walked the earth with a capital C, and probably a female form in light classic drapery. There was Felicity also. Iolo wrote 'Felicity, a pastoral.' He composed a poem to the cuckoo, and translated the famous Latin couplet which says that two pilgrimages to St David's are equivalent to one to Rome itself:

> " 'Would haughty Popes your senses bubble,
> And once to Rome your steps entice;
> 'Tis quite as well, and saves some trouble,
> Go visit old Saint Taffy twice.'

He wrote quantities of hymns. Once, to get some girls out of a scrape—one having played 'The Voice of Her I Love' on the organ after service—he wrote a hymn to the tune, 'The Voice of the Beloved,' and fathered it on an imaginary collection of Moravian hymns. One other virtue he had, as a bard: he never repeated his own verses. God rest his soul. He was a walker, not a writer. The best of him—in fact, the real man altogether—refused to go into verse at all.

"Yet he had peculiarities which might have adorned a poet. Once, when he was on a job in a churchyard at Dartford, his master told him to go next morning to take certain measurements. He went, and, having taken the measurements, *woke*. It was pitch dark, but soon afterwards a clock struck two. In spite of the darkness he had not only done what he had to do, but he said that on his way to the churchyard every object appeared to him as clear as by day. The measurements were correct.

"One night, asleep in his char, three women appeared to him, one with a mantle over her head. There was a sound like a gun, and one of the others fell, covered in blood. Next day, chance took him—was it chance?—into a farm near Cowbridge where he was welcomed by three women, one hooded in a shawl. Presently a young man entered with a gun, and laid it on the table, pointing at one of the women. At Iolo's warning it was discovered that the gun was primed and at full cock.

"Another time, between Cowbridge and Flimstone, he hesitated thrice at a stile, and then, going over, was just not too late to save a drunken man from a farmer galloping down the path.

"In spite of his love of Light and Liberty, he was not above turning necromancer with wand and magic circle to convert a sceptic inn-keeper. He undertook to call up the man's grandfather, and after some gesticulations and muttering unknown words, he whispered, 'I feel the approaching spirit. Shall it appear?' The man whom he was intending to benefit became alarmed, and begged to be allowed to hear the ghost speak, first of all. In a moment a deep, sepulchral voice pronounced the name of the grandfather. The man had had enough. He bolted from the place, leaving Iolo and his confederates triumphant.

"Iolo should have been content to leave it unproved that he was no poet. But he had not an easy life, and I suppose he had to have frills of some sort.

"Well, he walked home to Glamorgan. There he took a Glamorgan wife, Margaret Roberts of Marychurch, and he had to read less and work more to provide for a family. By the nature of his handiwork he was able to make more out of his verses than he would have done by printing better poetry. The vile doggerel which he inscribed on tombstones gained him a living and a sort of an immortality. He was one of the masons employed on the monument to the Man of Ross.

"Though a bad poet he was a Welsh bard. It was not the first or the last occasion on which the two parts were combined. Bard, for him, was a noble name. He was a 'Christian Briton and Bard'—a 'Bard according to the rights and institutes of the Bards of the Island of Britain'—and he never forgot the bardic triad, 'Man, Liberty, and Light.' Once, at the prison levee of a dissenting minister, he signed himself, 'Bard of Liberty.' To Southey, whom he helped with much out-of-the-way bardic mythology for his 'Madoc,' he was 'Bard Williams.'

"Bardism brought him into strange company, which I dare say he did not think strange, and certainly not absurd. Anna Seward, who mistook herself for a poet, and was one of the worst poets ever denominated 'Swan,' was kind to him in London. He in return initiated her into the bardic order at a meeting of 'Ancient British Bards resident in London,' which was convened on Primrose Hill at the Autumnal equinox, 1793. At an earlier meeting, also on Primrose Hill, he had recited an 'Ode on the Mythology of the British Bards in the manner of Taliesin,' and, since this poem was subsequently approved at the equinoctial, and ratified at the solstitial, convention, it was, according to ancient usage, fit for publication. It was not a reason. Nevertheless, a bard is a bard, whatever else he may or may not be.

"Iolo was proud to declare that the old Welsh bards had kept up a perpetual war with the church of Rome, and had suffered persecution. 'Man, Liberty, and Light.' You and I, Mr Stodham, perhaps don't know what he meant. But if Iolo did not know, he was too happy to allow the fact to emerge and trouble him.

"Of course, he connected the bards with Druidism, which he said they had kept alive. A good many sectarians would have said that he himself was as much a Druid as a Christian. He accepted the resurrection of the dead. He did not reject the Druid belief in transmigration of souls. He identified Druidism with the patriarchal religion of the Old Testament, but saw in it also a pacific and virtually Christian spirit. He affirmed that Ancient British Christianity was strongly tinctured by Druidism, and it was his opinion that the 'Dark Ages' were only dark through our lack of light. He hated the stories of Cæsar and others about human sacrifices, and would say to opponents, 'You are talking of what you don't understand—of what none but a Welshman and a British bard *can possibly* understand.' He compared the British mythology favourably with the 'barbarous' Scandinavian mythology of Thor and Odin. He studied whatever he could come at concerning Druidism, with the 'peculiar bias and firm persuasion' that 'more wisdom and beneficence than is popularly attributed to them' would be revealed.

"In the French Revolution he recognised the spirit of 'Man, Liberty, and Light.' His friends deserted him. He in turn was willing to leave them for America, 'to fly from the numerous injuries he had received from the laws of this land.' He had, furthermore, the hope of discovering the colony settled in America, as some believed, by the mediæval Welsh prince Madoc."

"That was like Borrow, too," suggested Mr Stodham.

"It was, and the likeness is even closer; for, like Borrow, Iolo did not go to America. Nevertheless, to prepare himself for the adventure, he lived out of doors for a time, sleeping in trees and on the ground, and incurring rheumatism.

"But though he did not go to America for love of Liberty, he had his papers seized, and is said to have been summoned by Pitt for disaffection to the State. Nothing worse was proved against him than the authorship of several songs in favour of Liberty, 'perhaps,' said his biographer, 'a little more extravagant than was quite commendable at that inflammatory period.' They expected him to remove his papers himself, but he refused, and had them formally restored by an official. When he was fifty he gave up his trade because the dust of the stone was injuring his lungs. He now earned a living by means of a shop at Cowbridge where books, stationery, and grocery were sold. His speciality was 'East India Sweets uncontaminated by human gore.' Brothers of his who had made money in Jamaica offered to allow him £50 a year, but in vain. 'It was a land of slaves,' he said. He would not even administer their property when it was left to him, though a small part was rescued later on by friends, for his son and daughter. The sound of the bells at Bristol celebrating the rejection of Wilberforce's Anti-Slavery Bill drove him straight out of the city. Believing that he was spied upon at Cowbridge he offered a book for sale in his window, labelled 'The Rights of Man.' He was successful. The spies descended on him, seized the book, and discovered that it was the Bible, not the work of Paine.

"He was personally acquainted with Paine and with a number of other celebrities, such as Benjamin Franklin, Bishop Percy, Horne Tooke, and Mrs Barbauld. Once in a bookshop he asked Dr Johnson to choose for him among three English grammars. Johnson was turning over the leaves of a book, 'rapidly and as the bard thought petulantly': 'Either of them will do for you, young man,' said he. 'Then, sir,' said Iolo, thinking Johnson was insulting his poverty, 'to make sure of having the best I will buy all'; and he used always to refer to them as 'Dr Johnson's Grammars.' It was once arranged that he should meet Cowper, but the poet sat, through the evening, silent, unable to encounter the introduction.

"The excesses of the Revolution, it is said, drove Iolo to abandon the idea of a Republic, except as a 'theoretic model for a free government.' He even composed an ode to the Cowbridge Volunteers. Above all, he wrote an epithalamium on the marriage of George the Fourth, which he himself presented, dressed in a new apron of white leather and carrying a bright trowel. His 'English Poems' were dedicated to the Prince of Wales."

"What a fearful fall," exclaimed Mr Stodham, who may himself have been a Bard of Liberty.

"But his business, apart from his trade, was antiquities, and especially the quest of them up and down Wales."

"I shouldn't be surprised," said Mr Stodham, "if the old man hoped for some grand result from meddling with those mysterious old books and papers—perhaps nothing definite, health, wealth, wisdom, beauty, everlasting life, or the philosopher's stone,—but some old secret of Bardism or Druidism, which would glorify Wales, or Cowbridge, or Old Iolo himself."

"Very likely. He was to a scientific antiquary what a witch is to an alchemist, and many a witch got a reputation with less to her credit than he had.

"As a boy he remembered hearing an old shoemaker of Llanmaes (near Lantwit) speak of the shaft of an ancient cross, in Lantwit churchyard, falling into a grave that had been dug too near it for Will the Giant of Lantwit. As a middle-aged man he dug up the stone. It was less love of antiquity than of mystery, buried treasure, and the like. He was unweariable in his search for the remains of Ancient British literature. At the age of seventy, when the Bishop of St David's had mislaid some of his manuscripts and they had thus been sold, Iolo walked over Caermarthenshire, Pembrokeshire, and Cardiganshire, and recovered the greater part. He took a pony with him as far as Caermarthen, but would not allow it to carry his wallets until at last it was arranged that his son should walk on one side and himself on the other, which made him remark that 'nothing was more fatiguing than a horse.' The horse appears in a triad of his own composition:

"There are three things I do not want. A Horse, for I have a good pair of legs: a Cellar, for I drink no beer: a Purse, for I have no money.

"He would not ride in Lord Dunraven's carriage, but preferred to walk. That he did not dislike the animal personally is pretty clear. For at one time he kept a horse which followed him, of its own free will, upon his walks.

"Iolo was a sight worth seeing on the highways and byways of

Glamorgan, and once had the honour of being taken for a conjuror. His biographer—a man named Elijah Waring, who was proud to have once carried his wallets—describes him 'wearing his long grey hair flowing over his high coat collar, which, by constant antagonism, had pushed up his hatbrim into a quaint angle of elevation behind. His countenance was marked by a combination of quiet intelligence and quick sensitiveness; the features regular, the lines deep, and the grey eye benevolent but highly excitable. He was clad, when he went to see a bishop, in a new coat fit for an admiral, with gilt buttons and buff waistcoat, but, as a rule, in rustic garb: the coat blue, with goodly brass buttons, and the nether integuments, good homely corduroy. He wore buckles in his shoes, and a pair of remarkably stout well-set legs were vouchers for the great peripatetic powers he was well known to possess. A pair of canvas wallets were slung over his shoulders, one depending in front, the other behind. These contained a change of linen, and a few books and papers connected with his favourite pursuits. He generally read as he walked. . . .'"

"Tut, tut," remarked Mr Stodham, "that spoils all."

"He generally read as he walked, 'with spectacles on nose,' and a pencil in his hand, serving him to make notes as they suggested themselves. Yet he found time also, Mr Stodham, to sow the tea-plant on the hills of Glamorgan. 'A tall staff which he grasped at about the level of his ear completed his equipment; and he was accustomed to assign as a reason for this mode of using it, that it tended to expand the pectoral muscles, and thus, in some degree, relieve a pulmonary malady inherent in his constitution.'

"He did not become a rich man. Late one evening he entered a Cardiganshire public-house and found the landlord refusing to let a pedlar pay for his lodging in kind, though he was penniless. Iolo paid the necessary shilling for a bed and rated the landlord, but had to walk on to a distant friend because it was his last shilling. Yet he wrote for the *Gentleman's Magazine* and corresponded with the *Monthly* and others, so that towards the end he was entitled to advances from the Literary Fund. An annual subscription was also raised for him in Neath and the neighbourhood. His last three

113

years he spent at Flimstone, where he is buried. He was a cripple and confined to the house, until one day he rested his head on the side of his easy chair and told his daughter that he was free from pain and could sleep, and so he died."

"I will certainly go to Craig-y-Dinas," said Mr Stodham solemnly, "and to Penon, and to Cowbridge, and to Flimstone."

"You will do well," said Mr Morgan, shutting up Elijah Waring's little book and getting out the map of Glamorgan.

CHAPTER XIV

THE CASTLE OF LEAVES AND THE BEGGAR
WITH THE LONG WHITE BEARD

ANN was good to all beggars as well as to old Jack, the watercress man, and when I asked her about it once she told the story of the Castle of Leaves. This castle was a ruin above the sea near where she was born. So fragmentary and fallen was it that every November the oak leaves covered it up. As a little child, Ann was taken up there on a May day because the hawthorn growing there always blossomed in time, however backward the season. Sitting among the ruins was an old white-haired man playing on a harp, and for ever after she loved beggars, said Aurelius, as if they were all going to have harps and long white beards in due course. A white-haired beggar, according to tradition, was infallibly to be found by anyone who went up to the Castle of Leaves on May day, and the story which connects a beggar with the early days of the castle might of itself explain why Ann never denied a beggar. Both Mr Morgan and Ann knew the story, but Mr Morgan had found it written in a book, with the date 1399, while Ann told it without a date as she remembered it from the dark ages of her own childhood.

In those old days, if Ann was to be believed, there was nothing but war. The young men went out to battle and never came back except as spirits, or as old men, or as worse than either—some of them having no more legs or arms than a fish, some crawling on their bellies with their beards in the mud, or flapping along in the wind like a kind of bird, or as lean and scattered as crickets—so that the children laughed at them first and then ran away crying to their mothers because they had such fathers. The mothers did not laugh save those that went mad, and perhaps they were not the worst off. The women knew that these strange idols and images crawling and jiggering home were the same that had marched out to the war as if their sweethearts were in the far countries before

115

them, instead of behind them at the turnings of the roads. They would not have loved them so much if they had not gone out like that. The glorious young men departed; the young women were no longer beautiful without them; the little children were blossoms of the grave. The world was full of old men, maimed men, and young men going to the wars, and of women crying because the soldiers had not come back, and children crying because they had. And many and many a one had no more tears left to cry with.

Beggars appeared and disappeared who looked like men, but spoke all manner of tongues and knew not where their fathers or mothers or children were, if they had any left, or if ever they had any, which was doubtful, for they were not as other men, but as if they had come thus into the astonished world, resembling carrion walking, or rotten trees by the roadside. Few could till the fields, and it was always a good summer for thistles, never for corn. The cattle died and there was nothing to eat the grass. Some said it was a judgment. But what had the poor cows and sheep done? What had the young men and women done? They were but mankind. Nor were the great ones the worse for it. They used to come back from the wars with gold and unicorns and black slaves carrying elephants' tusks and monkeys. Whether or not it was a judgment, it was misery.

But one day there was a white ship in the harbour of Abercorran. A man named Ivor ap Cadogan had come back who had been away in Arabia, Cathay, and India, in Ophir and all the East, since he was a boy. No man knew his family. He was a tall man with yellow hair and a long beard of gold, and he was always singing to himself, and he was like a king who has thrown away his crown, nor had he soldiers with him, but only the dark foreign men who followed him from the ships. All day long, day after day, they were unlading and carrying up beautiful white stone from the ship to build a great shining castle above the sea. In a little while came another ship out of the east, and another, and another, like swans, coming in silent to the harbour. All were heavy laden with the white stone, and with precious woods, which men carried up into the hills above the shore. The sea forgot everything but calm all through that summer while they were unlading the ships and building.

The finished castle was as huge and white, but not as terrible, as a mountain peak when the snow has been chiselled by the north wind for many midnights, and the wood of it smelt round about as sweet as a flower, summer and winter. And Ivor ap Cadogan dwelt in the castle, which was at that time called the Castle of Ophir. It had no gates, no moat or portcullis, for no one was refused or sent away. Its fires never went out. Day and night in winter the sky over the castle was bright with the many fires and many lights. Round the walls grew trees bearing golden fruit, and among them fountains of rustling crystal stood up glittering for ever like another sort of trees.

People dreamed about the shining, white castle, and its gold, its music, its everlasting festivals of youths and maidens.

Upon the roads now there were no more incomplete or withered men, or if they were they were making for the Castle of Ophir among the hills. It was better, said all men, to be a foreigner, or a monkey, or any one of the wondrous beasts that wandered in the castle, or any of the birds that flew round the towers, or any of the fish in the ponds under the fountains, than to be a man upon the roads or in the villages. No man now walked up and down until he had to sit, or sat until he had to lie, or lay until he could rise no more and so died. They went up to the Castle of Ophir and were healed, and dwelt there happily for ever after. Those that came back said that in the castle they were just as happy whether they were working hard or doing nothing: stiff, labouring men whose chief pleasure used to be in resting from toil, could be idle and happy in the castle long after their toil had been forgotten. The charcoal-burners slept until they were clean, and the millers until they were swarthy, and it seemed to them that the lives of their fathers had been a huddle of wretchedness between birth and death. Even the young men ceased going to the wars, but went instead to the castle and the music and the feasting. All men praised Ivor ap Cadogan. Once a lord from beyond the mountains sent men against the castle to carry off gold, but they remained with Ivor and threw their weapons into the ponds.

From time to time the white ships put out again from Abercorran, and again returned. When their sails appeared in the bay, it was known that calm had settled upon the sea as in the first year, and men and women went down to welcome them. Those summers were good both for man and beast. The earth brought forth tall, heavy corn which no winds beat down. Granaries were full: at the castle a granary, as large as a cathedral, was so full that the rats and mice had no room and so threw themselves into the sea. And Ivor ap Cadogan grew old. His beard was as white as the sails of his ships. A great beard it was, not like those of our day, and you could see it blowing over his shoulder a mile away as he walked the hills. So some men began to wonder whether one day he would die, and who would be master then, and whether it would still be calm when the ships sailed. But Summer came, and with it the ships, and Autumn and the cramming of granaries and the songs of harvest, and men forgot.

The next Summer was more glorious than any before. Only, the ships never came. The sea was quiet as the earth, as blue as the sky. The white clouds rose up out of the sea, but never one sail. Ivor went to the high places to watch, and lifted a child upon his shoulders to watch for him. No ship came. Ivor went no more to the cliffs, but stayed always on the topmost towers of the castle, walking to and fro, watching, while down below men were bringing in the harvest and the songs had begun.

When at last the west wind blew, and one ship arrived, it was not in the harbour but on the rocks, and it was full of dead men. Ivor and all the people of the castle went down to see the ship and the dead men. When they returned at nightfall the wind had blown the leaves from the castle trees into the rooms so that they were almost filled. The strange birds of the castle were thronging the air, in readiness to fly over the sea. The strange animals of the castle had left their comfort and were roaming in the villages, where they were afterwards killed. The old men prophesied terrible things. The women were afraid. The children stood, pale and silent, watching the dead leaves swim by like fishes, crimson and emerald and gold, and they pretended that they were mermen and mermaids sitting in a palace under the sea. But the women took the children away along the road where the old men had already gone. Led by Ivor, the young men descended to the shore to repair the ship.

It was a winter of storm: men could not hear themselves speak for the roaring of sea, wind, and rain, and the invisible armies of the air. With every tide bodies of men and of the strange birds that had set out over the sea were washed up. Men were not glad to see Ivor and his dark companions at last departing in the mended ship. The granaries were full, and no one starved, but time passed and no more ships arrived. No man could work. The castle stood empty of anything but leaves, and in their old cottages men did not love life. The Spring was an ill one; nothing was at work in the world save wind and rain; now the uproar of the wind drowned that of the rain, now the rain drowned the wind, and often the crying of women and children drowned both. Men marked the differences, and hoped for an end which they were powerless to pursue. When the one ship returned, its cargo was of birds and beasts such as had escaped in the falling of the leaves. Ivor alone was glad of them. He had few followers—young men all of them—up to the castle. Others came later, but went down again with loads of corn. It was now seen that the granaries would some day be emptied. People began to talk without respect of Ivor. They questioned whence his wealth had come, by what right he had built the castle, why he had concealed his birth. The young men living with him quarrelled among themselves, then agreed in reproaching the master. At last they left the castle in twos and threes, accusing him of magic, of causing them to forget their gratitude to God. In the villages everyone was quarrelling except when the talk turned to blaming Ivor. He made no reply, nor ever came down amongst them, but stayed in the inmost apartment with his remaining birds. One of the complaints against him was that he fed the birds on good grain. Yet the people continued to go up to the granaries at need. The beggars and robbers of the mountains were beginning to contest

119

their right to it, and blood was shed in many of the rooms and corridors. No one saw the master. They said that they did not care, or they said that he was dead and buried up in leaves; but in truth they were afraid of his white hair, his quiet eye, and the strange birds and beasts. Between them, the robbers and the young men who had served him plundered the house. Some even attempted to carry off the masonry, but left most of it along the roadside where it lies to this day. At length, nothing worth a strong man's time had been overlooked. A few beggars were the latest visitors, cursing the empty granary, trembling at the footsteps of leaves treading upon leaves in all the rooms. They did not see Ivor, sitting among leaves and spiders' webs. A pack of hounds, hunting that way, chased the stag throughout the castle but lost it; for it entered the room where Ivor was sitting, and when the horn was blown under the new moon the hounds slunk out bloodless yet assuaged, and the hunter thrashed them for their lack of spirit, and cursed the old man for his magic, yet ventured not in search of him along those muffled corridors. The very road up to the castle was disappearing. The master, it was believed, had died. The old men who had known him were dead; the young men were at the wars. When a white-haired beggar stumbled into Abercorran from the hills few admitted, though all knew in their hearts, that it was Ivor ap Cadogan. For a year or two he was fed from door to door, but he wearied his benefactors by talking continually about his birds that he had lost. Some of the rich remembered against him his modesty, others his ostentation. The poor accused him of pride; such was the name they gave to his independent tranquillity. Perhaps, some thought, it was a judgment—the inhabitants of the Castle of Ophir had been too idle and too happy to think of the shortness of this life and the glory to come. So he disappeared. Probably he went to some part where he was not known from any other wandering beggar. "Wonderful long white beards," said Ann, "men had in those days—longer than that old harper's, and to-day there are none even like him. Men to-day can do a number of things which the old ages never dreamed of, but their beards are nothing in comparison to those unhappy old days when men with those long white beards used to sit by the roadsides, looking as if they had come from the ends of the earth, like wise men from the East, although they were so old that they sat still with their beards reaching to the ground like roots. Ivor ap Cadogan was one of these."

Mr Morgan once, overhearing Ann telling me this tale, said, "What the book says is much better. It says that in 1399 a Welshman, named Llewelyn ab Cadwgan, who would never speak of his family, came from the Turkish war to reside at Cardiff; and so great was his wealth that he gave to everyone that asked or could be seen to be in need of it. He built a large mansion near the old white tower, for the support of the sick and infirm. He continued to give all that was asked of him until his wealth was all gone. He then sold his house, which was called the New Place, and gave away the money until that also was at an end. After this he died of want, for no one gave to him, and many accused him of extravagant waste." With that Mr Morgan went gladly and, for him, rapidly to his books. Nobody seeing him then was likely to disturb him for that evening. At his door he turned and said "Good night" to us in a perfectly kind voice which nevertheless conveyed, in an unquestionable manner, that he was not to be disturbed.

"Good night, Mr Morgan," said all of us. "Good night, Ann," said I, and slipped out into a night full of stars and of quietly falling leaves, which almost immediately silenced my attempt to sing "O the cuckoo is a pretty bird" on the way home.

CHAPTER XV

SOME time after the story of the Castle of Leaves, Mr Morgan took occasion to point out the difference between Ann speaking of the "beautiful long white beards" that men grew in those "unhappy old days," and Mr Torrance praising the "merry" or "good old" England of his imagination. He said that from what he could gather they were merry in the old days with little cause, while to-day, whatever cause there might be, few persons possessed the ability. He concluded, I think, that after all there was probably nothing to be merry about at any time if you looked round carefully: that, in fact, what was really important was to be capable of more merriment and less ado about nothing. Someone with a precocious sneer, asked if England was now anything more than a geographical expression, and Mr Stodham preached a sermon straight away:

"A great poet said once upon a time that this earth is 'where we have our happiness or not at all.' For most of those who speak his language he might have said that this England is where we have our happiness or not at all. He meant to say that we are limited creatures, not angels, and that our immediate surroundings are enough to exercise all our faculties of mind and body: there is no need to flatter ourselves with the belief that we could do better in a bigger or another world. Only the bad workman complains of his tools.

"There was another poet who hailed England, his native land, and asked how could it but be dear and holy to him, because he declared himself one who (here Mr Stodham grew very red and his voice rose, and Lewis thought he was going to sing as he recited):

"'From thy lakes and mountain-hills,
Thy clouds, thy quiet dales, thy rocks and seas,

122

Have drunk in all my intellectual life,
All sweet sensations, all ennobling thoughts,
All adoration of the God in nature,
All lovely and all honourable things,
Whatever makes this mortal spirit feel
The joy and greatness of its future being?
There lives nor form nor feeling in my soul
Unborrowed from my country. O divine
And beauteous island! thou hast been my sole
And most magnificent temple, in the which
I walk with awe, and sing my stately songs,
Loving the God that made me!'

"Of course, I do not know what it *all* means," he muttered, but went on: "and that other poet who was his friend called the lark:

" 'Type of the wise who soar but never roam,
True to the kindred points of heaven and home.'

Well, England is home and heaven too. England made you, and of you is England made. Deny England—wise men have done so— and you may find yourself some day denying your father and mother—and this also wise men have done. Having denied England and your father and mother, you may have to deny your own self, and treat it as nothing, a mere conventional boundary, an artifice, by which you are separated from the universe and its creator. To unite yourself with the universe and the creator, you may be tempted to destroy that boundary of your own body and brain, and die. He is a bold man who hopes to do without earth, England, family, and self. Many a man dies, having made little of these things, and if he says at the end of a long life that he has had enough, he means only that he has no capacity for more—*he* is exhausted, not the earth, not England.

"I do not think that a man who knows many languages, many histories, many lands, would ask if England was more than a geographical expression. Nor would he be the first to attempt an answer to one that did ask.

"I do not want you to praise England. She can do without receiving better than you can without giving. I do not want to shout that our great soldiers and poets are greater than those of other nations, but they are ours, they are great, and in proportion as we are good and intelligent, we can respond to them and understand them as those who are not Englishmen cannot. They cannot long do without us or we without them. Think of it. We have each of us some of the blood and spirit of Sir Thomas More, and Sir Philip Sidney, and the man who wrote 'Tom Jones,' and Horatio Nelson, and the man who wrote 'Love in the Valley.' Think what we owe to them of joy, courage, and mere security. Try to think what they owe to us, since they depend on us for keeping alive their spirits, and a spirit that can value them. They are England: we are England. Deny England, and we deny them and ourselves. Do you love the Wilderness? Do you love Wales? If you do, you love what I understand by 'England.' The more you love and know England, the more deeply you can love the Wilderness and Wales. I am sure of it. . . ."

At this point Mr Stodham ran away. Nobody thought how like a *very good* rat he was during this speech, or, rather, this series of short speeches interrupted by moments of excitement when all that he could do was to light a pipe and let it out. Higgs, perhaps, came nearest to laughing; for he struck up "Rule Britannia" with evident pride that he was the first to think of it. This raised my gorge; I could not help shouting "Home Rule for Ireland." Whereupon Higgs swore abominably, and I do not know what would have happened if Ann had not said: "Jessie, my love, sing *Land of my Fathers*," which is the Welsh national anthem; but when Jessie sang it—in English, for our sakes—everyone but Higgs joined in the chorus and felt that it breathed the spirit of patriotism which Mr Stodham had been trying to express. It was exulting without self-glorification or any other form of brutality. It might well be the national anthem of any nation that knows, and would not rashly destroy, the bonds distinguishing it from the rest of the world without isolating it.

Aurelius, who had been brooding for some time, said:

"I should never have thought it. Mr Stodham has made me a present of a country. I really did not know before that England was not a shocking fiction of the journalists and politicians. I am the richer, and, according to Mr Stodham, so is England. But what about London fog? what is the correct attitude of a patriot towards London fog and the manufacturers who make it what it is?"

Aurelius got up to look out at the fog, the many dim trees, the single gas lamp in the lane beyond the yard. Pointing to the trees, he asked—

> " 'What are these,
> So withered and so wild in their attire,
> That look not like th' inhabitants o' the earth
> And yet are on't?'

Even so must Mr Stodham's patriotism, or that of *Land of our Fathers*, appear to Higgs. His patriotism is more like the 'Elephant and Castle' on a Saturday night than those trees. Both are good, as they say at Cambridge." And he went out, muttering towards the trees in the fog:

> " 'Live you? or are you aught
> That man may question? You seem to understand me,
> By each at once her choppy fingers laying
> Upon her skinny lips: you should be women,
> And yet your beards forbid me to interpret
> That you are so.' "

For some time we were all silent, until Ann said: "Hark." "What is it? another Ripper murder?" said Higgs. "Oh, shut up, Higgs," said Philip looking at Ann. "Hark," said Ann again. It was horrible. Somewhere far off I could hear an angry murmur broken by frantic metallic clashings. No one sound out of the devilish babble could I disentangle, still less, explain. A myriad noises were violently mixed in one muddy, struggling mass of rumbling and jangling. The worst gramophones are infinitely nearer to the cooing of doves than this, but it had in it something strained, reckless, drunken-mad, horror-stricken, like the voice of the gramophone. Above all, the babble was angry and it was inhuman. I had never heard it before, and my first thought was that it was an armed and furious multitude, perhaps a foreign invader, a mile or so distant.

"Didn't you know it was Saturday night?" said Higgs. "It is always worse on Saturdays."

"What is?" said I.

"That noise," said Higgs.

"Hark," said Philip anxiously, and we all held our breath to catch it again. There . . . It was no nearer. It was not advancing. It was always the same. As I realised that it was the mutter of London, I sighed, being a child, with relief, but could not help listening still for every moment of that roar as of interlaced immortal dragons fighting eternally in a pit. It was surprising that such a tone could endure. The sea sounds everlastingly, but this was more appropriate to a dying curse, and should have lasted no more than a few minutes. As I listened it seemed rather to be a brutish yell of agony during the infliction of some unspeakable pain, and though pain of that degree would kill or stupefy in a few minutes, this did not.

"If you like the 'Elephant and Castle,'" said Mr Morgan, "you like that. But if you live in London all your lives, perhaps you may never hear it again.

"For the sound does not cease. We help to make it as we do to make England. Even those weird sisters of Aurelius out in the Wilderness help to make it by rattling branches and dropping leaves in the fog. You will hear the leaves falling, the clock ticking, the fog-signals exploding, but not London."

I was, in fact, twenty-one before I heard the roar again. Neversince have I noticed it. But Ann, it seems, used to hear it continually, perhaps because she went out so seldom and could not become one of the mob of unquestionable "inhabitants o' the earth." But when the window had been shut, we, at any rate, forgot all about London in that warm room in Abercorran House, amidst the gleam of china and the glitter of brass and silver. Lewis and Harry sat on the floor, in a corner, playing with lead soldiers. The English army—that is to say, Lewis—was beaten, and refused to accept its fate. On being told, "But it is all over now," he burst out crying. Harry looked on in sympathetic awe. But before his tears had quite come to their natural end, a brilliant idea caused him to uncover his face suddenly and say: "I know what I shall do. I shall build a tower like David—a real one—in the Wilderness."

"Oh, yes, let's," exclaimed Harry.

"Us," said Lewis, "I like that. It is I that shall build a tower. But I will *employ* you."

"That," mused Harry slowly, "means that I build a tower and let you live in it. That isn't right. Mr Gladstone would never allow it."

"What has Mr Gladstone got to do with the Wilderness, I should like to know? We *employ* him. I should like to see him getting over the fence into the Wilderness. He does not know where it is. Besides, if he did, he could *never*, *never*, get into my tower. If he did I would immediately fling myself down from the top. Then I should be safe," shrieked Lewis, before entering another of those vales or abysses of tears which were so black for him, and so brief. It was not so agreeable as silence would have been, or as Ann's sewing was, or the continuous bagpipe music of a kettle always just on the boil. But Philip had gone upstairs, and the book on my knee held me more than Lewis's tears. This book placed me in a mountain solitude such as that where David Morgan had built his tower, and, like that, haunted by curlews:

> "The rugged mountain's scanty cloak
> Was dwarfish shrubs of birch and oak,
> With shingles bare, and cliffs between,
> And patches bright of bracken green,
> And heather black that waved so high
> It held the copse in rivalry."

Out of the ambush of copse and heather and bracken had started up at a chieftain's whistle—"wild as the scream of the curlew"—a host of mountaineers, while the chieftain revealed himself to the enemy who had imagined him alone:

> "And, Saxon, I am Roderick Dhu."

127

"What is the matter, Arthur?" asked Harry when I came to this line. I answered him with a look of trembling contempt. The whole scene so fascinated me—I so thrilled with admiration at everything done by the Highland chieftain—that his magic whistle at last pierced me to the marrow with exquisite joy. In my excitement I said the words, "And, Saxon, I am Roderick Dhu," aloud, yet not loud enough to make anything but a husky muttering audible. I was choking and blushing with pleasant pains and with a desire to pass them on to another, myself not lacking glory as the discoverer. Hence my muttering those words aloud: hence the contempt of my answer to Harry, upon not being instantly and enthusiastically understood. The contempt, however, was not satisfying. . . . I, too, wished that I possessed a tower upon a mountain where I could live for ever in a state of poetic pain. Therefore I went out silently, saying no good night, not seeing Philip again.

Fog and cold cured me rapidly. On that wretched night I could no more go on thinking of a tower on a mountain than I could jump into a pond. I had to run to get warm. Then I thought of the book once more: I recovered my pleasure and my pride. The fog, pierced by some feeble sparkles of lamps, and dim glows of windows from invisible houses, the silence, broken by the dead leaf that rustled after me, made the world a shadowy vast stage on which I was the one real thing. The solitary grandeur was better than any tower, and at the end of my run, on entering again among people and bright lights, I could flit out of it as easily as possible, which was more than Morgan could do, since to escape from his tower he had to die.

CHAPTER XVI

THE HOUSE OF THE DAYS OF THE YEAR

LEWIS never did raise a tower in the Wilderness. His towers were in the air. A wish, with him, was seldom father to any deed. I think he expected the wish of itself to create; or if not, he was at least always angered when the nature of things proved to be against him. He would not have been unduly astonished, and would have been wildly grateful, if he had seen looming through the fog next morning a tower such as he desired. But except on paper he never did. As he drew it, the tower was tall and slender as the tallest and slenderest factory chimney, more like a pillar for St Simeon Stylites than a castle in Spain. It would have been several times the height of the elms in the Wilderness which he had furiously refused to take into his service. It was to be climbed within by a spiral staircase, each step apparently having its own little window. Thus it was riddled by windows.

Now, if this idea had come to Philip he would have executed it. As it was, Lewis's drawing delighted him. He liked all those windows that made it look as if it were a dead stem rotting away. "But," said he, "I know a house better than that, with a window for every day of the year. It would be just the thing for you, Lewis, because it is built without hands, without bricks, stones, cement, or any expense whatever. . . . It was only a dream," he continued, one day as he and I were going down the long street which took us almost straight out into Our Country. But he did not really think it no more than a dream. He had seen it many times, a large, shadowy house, with windows which he had never counted, but knew to be as many as the days of the year, no more, no less. The house itself was always dark, with lights in some of the windows, never, perhaps, in all.

The strange thing was that Philip believed this house must

actually exist. Perhaps, I suggested, it was hidden among the trees of our woods, like several other houses. No: he dismissed this as fancy. His house was not a fancy. It lay somewhere in a great city, or at the verge of one. On his first visit he had approached it by long wanderings through innumerable, unknown and deserted streets, following a trail of white pebbles like the children in the fairy tale. In all those streets he passed nobody and heard no sound; nor did this surprise him, in spite of the fact that he felt the houses to be thronged with people. Suddenly out of the last narrow street he came as it were on a wall of darkness, like night itself. Into this he was stepping forward when he saw just beneath and before him a broad, black river, crossed by a low bridge leading over to where, high up, a light beamed in the window of an invisible building. When he began to cross the bridge he could see that it was the greatest house he had ever beheld. It was a house that might be supposed to contain "many mansions." "You could not make a house like that one out of this whole street," said Philip. "It stretched across the world, but it was a house." On the other side of the river it seemed still equally far off. Birds flying to and fro before it never rose up over it, nor did any come from the other side. Philip hastened forward to reach the house. But the one light went out and he awoke.

Philip used to look out for this house when he was crossing the bridges in London. He scanned carefully the warehouses and factories rising out of the water, in long rows with uncounted windows, that made him wonder what went on behind them. With this material, he said, a magician could make a house like the one he was in search of. Once, when he got home in the evening from London, he was confident that his house lay between Waterloo Bridge and Hungerford Bridge, but next time he was there he was dead against any such suggestion. A factory on the edge of a tract of suburb waste fulfilled his conditions for an hour at another time. He had been thrilled, too, by a photograph shown to him by Mr Stodham—of an ancient palace standing at the foot of a desolate mountain in the remote South.

When we were walking together towards the country Philip used to look, as a matter of course, down every side street to right or left, as he always looked up dark alleys in London. Nor was he content to look once down any one street, lest he should miss some transformation or transfiguration. As we began to get clear of London, and houses were fewer and all had long front gardens, and shops ceased, Philip looked ahead now and then as well as from side to side. Beyond the wide, level fields and the tall Lombardy poplars bounding them, there was nothing, but there was room for the house. Fog thickened early in the afternoon over our vacant territories, but we saw only the trees and a Gypsy tent under a hedge.

Next day Philip came home feverish from school, and was put to bed in the middle of the pale sunny afternoon. He lay happily stretched out with his eyes fixed on a glass of water near the window. It flickered in the light. . . . He saw the black river gleaming as when a candle for the first time illuminates a lake in the bowels of a mountain. There was the house beyond the river. Six or seven of its windows were lit up, one large one low down, the rest small, high up, and, except two of them, wide apart. Now and then, at other windows here and there, lights appeared momentarily, like stars uncovered by rapid clouds. . . . A lofty central door slowly swung open. A tiny figure, as solitary as the first star in the sky, paused at the threshold, to be swallowed up a moment later in darkness. At the same moment Philip awoke with a cry, knowing that the figure was himself.

After this Philip was not so confident of discovering the house. Yet he was more than ever certain that it existed, that all the time of the intervals between his visits it was somewhere. I told him the story about Irem Dhat El'Imad, the Terrestrial Paradise of Sheddad the son of Ad, King of the World, which Aurelius had read to me. Philip was pleased with the part where the geometricians and sages, labourers and artificers of the King search over all the earth, until they come to rivers and an illimitable plain, and choose it for the site of the palace which was three hundred years building. But he said that this story was not true. His own great house never disappeared, he said; it was *he* that disappeared. By this time he had become so familiar with the house that he probably passed hardly a day without a sight of it, sleeping or waking. He was familiar with its monotonous front, the many storeys of not quite regular diminishing windows. It always seemed to lie out beyond a tract of solitude, silence, and blackness; it was beyond the black river; it was at the edge of the earth. In none of his visits could he get round to the other side. Several times again, as on that feverish afternoon, he saw himself entering through the lofty doorway, never emerging. What *this* self (for so he called it, touching his breast) saw inside the door he never knew. That self which looked on could never reach the door, could not cross the space between it and the river, though it seemed of no formidable immensity. Many times he set out to cross and go in at the other door after the other self, but could not. Finally he used to imagine that if once he penetrated to the other side he would see another world.

Once or twice Philip and I found ourselves in streets which he thought were connected with his first journey, but he vainly tried to remember how. He even used to say that at a certain number— once it was 197—lived some one who could help. When another dream took him along the original route of streets he told me that they were now thronged with people going with or against him. They were still all about him as he emerged from the streets in sight of the house, where every window was blazing with lights as he had never seen it before. The crowd was making towards the light across the hitherto always desolate bridge. Nevertheless, beyond the river, in the space before the house, he was alone as before. He resolved to cross the space. The great door ahead was empty; no other self at least had the privilege denied to him. He stood still, looking not at the door, but at the windows and at the multitudes passing behind them. His eyes were fixed on the upper windows and on each face in turn that appeared. Some faces he recognised without being able to give a name to one. They must have been people whom he had encountered in the street, and forgotten and never seen again until now. Apparently not one of them saw him standing out there, in the darkness, looking up at them. He was separated from them as from the dead, or as a dead man might be from the living. The moment he lowered his head to look towards the door, the dream was over.

More than once afterwards, when Lewis had ceased to think of his tower, Philip saw the hundreds of windows burning in the night above the black river, and saw the stream of faces at the windows; but he gave up expecting to see the house by the light of our sun or moon. He had even a feeling that he would rather not discover it, that if he were to enter it and join those faces at the windows he might not return, never stand out in the dark again and look up at the house.

CHAPTER XVII

THAT winter when Philip was ill, for the first time, I used to spend every evening at Abercorran House, chiefly upstairs, reading aloud or talking. I was supposed to entertain him, but he did most of the entertaining. Out of his own head or out of books he told me hundreds of tales; in either case they were very much his own. I cannot imitate him. For example, he would always bring his characters before himself and his listener by comparing them to persons known to both. When he was well and out of doors he would pick out a man or woman passing us, or at a window, for a comparison. "This Palomides," he would say, "was like that butcher, but dressed differently: you could see what good legs he had." Another was "like my brother Roland, and if he had been alive now he could have jumped over spiked railings up to his own shoulder, though he was not a little man." The Icelandic Thorbeorg was "like our Jessie: only she would use a knife, and she had fair hair." A certain villain was "a scoundrel, *but* he had a face like Higgs." The man who resembled Roland was an Icelander, Haurd by name, whom Philip called Roland throughout the tale. Thorbeorg was his sister. This was the tale:

Haurd was a head taller than most men, and he had grand hair. He was clever, strong, and bold. He swam better than all others, and his eyesight was wonderful. But he was a touchy man. Not being asked in the proper manner to his sister Thurid's wedding feast, he refused to go when the bridegroom, Illuge, came on purpose to fetch him. Yet a little after, when Geir, his own foster-brother, asked him to go just to please him, he went. However, at the feast he treated Illuge lightly; refused the present of a shield—accepted a ring, but with the remark that in his opinion being a brother-in-law would not mean much to Illuge.

Hearing Haurd say such things in a lazy way for no apparent reason and taken aback by it, he did not answer. As soon as he got home, Haurd gave the ring to his sister, Thorbeorg, bidding her remember him when he was dead. Soon afterwards, with Geir and his other foster-brother, Helge, who was a tramp's son, he left home.

Twenty years before that, when Thorbeorg's mother Signy was married to Grimkel, her brother Torfe took offence in the same way, because he was not consulted. Signy was very fond of him, and it was at his house that she gave birth to Thorbeorg and died the same day. Grief for his sister made him hate the child; he cast it out of the house, and chance alone saved its life. Thus Grimkel had a quarrel with Torfe over Signy's marriage portion and the injury to his child, Thorbeorg.

Fifteen years Haurd stayed away from home. He got renown as a fighter. He won honour, wealth, and an earl's daughter, Helga, for a wife. This Helga was as noble a lady as Thorbeorg.

Geir was the first of the exiles to return. He went to take possession of the farm at Netherbottom, on the death of Grim, his father. Here now, with Geir, were living his old mother and Thorbeorg, Haurd's sister. Perhaps Geir wished to marry Thorbeorg, but he was not the king of men she wanted, though he was honest and feared nothing; so he did not win her. She preferred one named Eindride, who came wooing her once in Geir's absence. She was not in love with him, but her father, Grimkel, liked the match, amd maybe she expected to be freer. When the wedding was over Grimkel consulted a witch about the future. Whatever she answered, it was bad, and the old man died that evening. Until his son, Haurd, came back, Grimkel's property fell into the care of the two sons-in-law, Illuge and Eindride.

Haurd came back with Helge, with Sigrod his uncle, Torfe's foster-son, and thirty followers. The quarrel with Torfe and Illuge soon had an opportunity of growing. In a fit of anger Helge killed a boy for injuring a horse which belonged to Haurd. Haurd offered to atone for the crime to Ead, the boy's father, but too late. Torfe, replied the man, had already listened to his complaint and was taking up the case. At this, Haurd drew his sword in fury and

135

hewed the man in two and a servant with him. He burnt Ead's homestead, his stores, and two women who were afraid to come out of hiding.

Haurd would have liked to win over to his part his sister Thorbeorg's husband, Eindride, but instead of going himself he sent Helge. If a good man had come, said Thorbeorg afterwards, things might have turned out differently. Eindride excused himself on account of an engagement with Illuge; not content to let this end the matter, he suggested that Haurd should come over himself. Helge turned upon him and taunted him with being a craven if he would not break that engagement with Illuge, but Eindride had nothing to add. All that Helge brought back to Haurd was that Eindride offered no help.

Everyone being against them, Haurd and Helge were outlawed. They had to quit the homestead, and rather than leave it for Torfe, they burnt it and all the hay with it. They and the household took refuge at Geir's house, Netherbottom. From here they raided the country on every side, carrying off whatever they wanted. Before long men gathered together to subdue them. Geir was for making a fort against the attack. Haurd, fearing that they would be starved out, proposed retreating to an impregnable islet which lay not far from land by a river's mouth. Haurd prevailed and they took possession. The islet consisted of precipices surmounted by a single level platform, "not half the size of the Wilderness," from which one steep pathway led to the sea. With timber from Netherbottom, the outlaws built a hall in this platform; and it had underground passages. The islet was called Geir's Holm, and they raided from it as they had done before, both craftily and boldly. Once on the islet they were safe from any attack. "It was the very place for Lewis," said Philip; "only there was no water in it, and no food unless there were sea-gulls' eggs."

Many of the landless and outlawed men of Iceland attached themselves to Haurd and Geir, swearing to be faithful to these two and to one another, and to share in all labours. It was a law of Geir's Holm that if a man was ill more than three nights he was to be thrown over the cliffs. The most that were on the island at one time was two hundred, the least eighty. Haurd, Geir, Sigrod, Helge, Thord Colt, and Thorgar Girdlebeard, were the chief men. The cruellest of all was Thorgar, and the readiest for every kind of wrongdoing.

At last men met together to consider how they might stop the raiding. Thorbeorg would not be left behind by Eindride, though he warned her that she would hear nothing pleasant at the meeting. The crowd became silent as she entered, and she spoke immediately to some of the chief men. . . . Here, Philip got up out of bed looking very grim while he uttered the words of Thorbeorg: "I know what you want to do. Very good. I cannot stop you by myself. But this I can do, and will—I will be the death of the man who kills Haurd. . . ." Philip stood entranced and still as a statue at the window, as if he could see her so long as he remained still. His weakness, however, made him totter, and he got into bed, saying: "She was magnificent. I would have done anything for her. She said nothing else. She rode away without waiting for an answer." Torfe advised swift and violent measures against the Islanders, but when Ref suggested that someone should put them off their guard by pretending that they were free to go where they wished and be at peace with all men, he thought well of the plan: in fact he said they should ride that very night to a place out of sight of the Islanders. Next day they saw Thorgar and Sigrod with twelve other outlaws coming for water. Twice their number were sent against them. Thorgar and seven others ran away. He formed a band of his own and was only killed after a long freedom. Sigrod and those who were left made a hard fight, but all were killed.

It was not easy to get a man to go next day and play the traitor on the Holm, although Torfe declared that whoever went would have great honour. In the end, Ref's brother, Kiartan, offered to go, if he could have Haurd's ring for a reward. He took the boat of Thorstan Goldknop, both because he disliked that man and because, being his, it would not excite suspicion. The story he told the outlaws was that, chiefly through Illuge and his friends, it had been decided that they should be free to go where they wished and have peace. If they agreed, he himself would row them ashore.

Geir believed Kiartan, especially as he came in the boat of one who was sworn never to betray them. Many others also were eager to leave. But Haurd thought that Kiartan did not look like a man who was bringing good, and he said so. Kiartan offered to swear that he was speaking truth, and still Haurd told him that he had the eyes of a man whose word was not worth much. Haurd did not hide his doubts. Nevertheless, a full boat-load went off with Kiartan, talking cheerfully. They were landed out of sight of the Holm, and every one of them was penned in and killed on the spot.

Kiartan returned for a second load. In spite of Haurd's advice, Geir now entered the boat. So many followed him that only six were left with Haurd and Helga and their two sons, and Helge, Haurd's foster-brother. Haurd was sad to see the boat going, and Geir and his companions were silent. When they rounded the spit, out of sight of those on the Holm, they saw the enemy waiting. Close to land Geir sprang overboard and swam out along the rocks. A man of Eindride's company struck him with a javelin between the shoulders, and he died. This Helga saw sitting on the Holm; but Haurd, who was with her, saw differently. The rest were penned in and butchered.

A third time Kiartan rowed out. Haurd bantered him for a ferryman who was doing a good trade, but still stuck to the opinion that he was not a true man. If Kiartan had not taunted him with being afraid to follow his men, Haurd would never have gone in that boat. Helga would not go, nor let her sons go. She wept over her husband as a doomed man. Once the boat had put out he was angry with himself. When they came alongside the rocks and saw the dead body of Geir, Haurd stood up in the boat and clove Kiartan down as far as the girdle with his sword. The men on shore made friendly signs to the last, but as soon as the boat touched land all were made prisoners except Haurd, who refused to be taken until he had slain four men. Eindride, who first laid hands on him, remembering what Thorbeorg had promised her brother's murderer, held out the axe for someone else to slaughter him; but no one would; and it was Haurd himself that seized the axe, for he burst his bonds. Helge followed, and they got away, though the ring of enemies was three deep. Haurd would never have been overtaken, though Ref was on horseback, if a spell had not been cast on him: moreover, Helge began to limp with a fearful wound. Even so, Haurd again broke through them, killing three more. Ref again caught him, yet dared not meddle with him, though he now had Helge on his back, until the others made a ring about him with the aid of a spell. There was nothing for it but to drop Helge and save him from his enemies by killing him. Haurd was enraged because he knew that a spell was being used on him; he was so fearful to look at that no one would go for him until Torfe had promised Haurd's ring to the man who did. Almost a dozen set on him together to earn the ring. Six of them had fallen before him when the head flew off his axe; nor did any one venture even then to close with him. From behind, however, Thorstan Goldknop, a big red-headed man, but mean, swung at his neck with an axe; so that he died. He had killed sixteen men altogether. Even his enemies said now that Haurd—Philip, in tears, said Roland, not Haurd—had been the bravest man of his time. If he had not had rogues among his followers he would have been living yet; but he never had been a lucky man. Thorstan got his ring. At that time he had not heard of Thorbeorg's vow; when he did hear he took no pleasure in the ring.

Sixty of the Islanders had been slain. All the rest had escaped, except Helga, and the two sons of Helga and Haurd, who had stayed on the island. It was too late to fetch away those three that evening, and before the sunrise next day they also had escaped. Under cover of darkness the mother swam over first with Beorn, who was four, and next with Grimkel, who was eight. Then carrying Beorn and leading Grimkel by the hand, Helga climbed over the hills until they came to Eindride's house. Under the fence of the yard, Helga sank down with Beorn. Grimkel she sent up to Thorbeorg to ask her to save them. Haurd's sister was sitting alone at the end of the hall, looking so grand and stern that the child stopped still without a word. "She was like a great queen of sorrows," said Philip, "but she had to come down to him." She led him outside to the light, she picked him up to take a good look at him, she asked who he was. He told her that he was Haurd's son.

She asked him where his mother was, and what had happened. He told her what he could while they were walking down to the fence. The sister and the wife of Haurd looked at one another. Thorbeorg gave the three a hiding place in an out-house, and herself took the key. Not long afterwards Eindride came home with a number of men. Thorbeorg served a meal for them, and they related all that had happened; but she said nothing until one of them told how Thorstan Goldknop had struck Haurd from behind when he was unarmed. "He was no better than a hangman or a butcher," said Philip. Thorbeorg cried that she knew a spell had been cast on her brother, or they would never have overcome him. That night as they were going to bed Thorbeorg made a thrust at Eindride with a knife, but wounded him in the hand only. He asked her if anything he could do now would satisfy her. "The head of Thorstan Goldknop," she replied. Next morning Eindride slew Thorstan and brought back the head. "He deserved it," said Philip, "and Thorbeorg kept her vow." Still she was not satisfied. She refused to make peace with her husband unless he would befriend Helga and her sons, should they need it. Eindride, supposing that they had been drowned, readily promised to do what she asked. Thorbeorg showed him his mistake. She went out, and came back, leading Helga and the two boys. Eindride was sorry, because he had sworn already not to do anything for Haurd's family, but he had to keep his oath to Thorbeorg. Nor did men blame him, and they praised Thorbeorg. Still she was not satisfied. Twenty-four men died in the next months because of Haurd, and most of them at her instiga-tion. She and Eindride lived on after that in peace to a great age, leaving behind them good children and grandchildren, who in their turn had many brave and honourable descendants. "I am sorry," said Philip, "that Haurd got that blow from behind. But he was a man who had to make a story before he died. And if this had not happened Thorstan might have gone on living, and have missed his due. Also perhaps Thorbeorg would not have had a chance of showing what she was good for. Now it is all over. They are put in a tale. I don't know what happened to Torfe and Illuge, but everyone who hears the story either hates them or forgets them:

so they have *their* reward. If Grimkel and Beorn lived to be men, I am sure Torfe and Illuge did not die in their beds."

With a deep sigh Philip stopped. For some minutes he said nothing. When he broke his silence it was to say: "Perhaps Roland will really do something like Haurd. He looks like it. He could. Don't you think he is one of those people who look as if men would some day have to tell stories of them to one another? *He* would not build a tower up on a mountain for nothing, and live there no better than a man could live at Clapham Junction." Here Philip cried, which I never saw him do before or after that day. It was the beginning of the worst part of his illness. Not for many weeks was he out of bed, and once more any companion in the house, in the yard, in Our Country, or at school on those rare days when he attended.

CHAPTER XVIII

WHAT WILL ROLAND DO?

ROLAND and Jack were too much my seniors, and yet still too young, to take notice of me. But I could admire them from afar for their gifts and opportunities, their good looks, their bodily prowess, liberty, and apparent lack of all care. Their activities were mostly away from home, and rumours, probably, were incomplete. Roland ran and jumped at sports, rode a horse, sometimes into the yard, sometimes out to where the fox was hunted (a little beyond *our* range)—bicycled hither and thither—possessed a gun and used it, doubtless in a magnificent manner—dressed as he should be dressed—was more than once in trouble of some kind, I think in debt, and had once been observed by me in London walking with a dark lady of his own splendid breed, whom I never heard anything of, or saw again. What I first knew of Roland was—shortly after I began to frequent Abercorran House—a voice singing mightily in the bathroom:

> "Foul fall the hand that bends the steel
> Around the courser's thundering heel,
> That e'er shall print a sable wound
> On fair Glamorgan's velvet ground."

Never afterwards did he do anything that fell short of the name Roland, to which the noble war-song, at that moment, fixed its character for ever. Jack and he had been to a famous school until they were sixteen, and did no good there. Indoors they learnt very little more than a manner extremely well suited to hours of idleness. Out of doors they excelled at the more selfish sports, at athletics, boxing, sculling, shooting. So they had come home and,

142

as Mr Morgan had nothing to suggest, they had done what suggested itself.

You could see Mr Morgan thinking as he watched the two, undecided whether it was best to think with or without the cigar, which he might remove for a few seconds, perhaps without advantage, for it was replaced with evident satisfaction. But he was thinking as he stood there, pale, rigid, and abstracted. Then perhaps Roland would do or say something accompanied by a characteristic free, bold, easy gesture, turning on his heel; and the father gave up thinking, to laugh heartily, and as likely as not step forward to enter the conversation, or ask Roland about the dogs, or what he had been doing in this past week. "Had a good time? . . . suits you? . . . Ha, ha, . . . Well, this will never do, I must be going. Good-bye, good-bye. Don't forget to look in and see how mother is."

He had only gone upstairs to the Library to open one of the new reviews which, except where they caught the sunshine, remained so new. He and his two elder sons always parted with a laugh. Either he manoeuvred for it, or as soon as the good laugh arrived he slipped away lest worse might befall. He saw clearly enough that "they had no more place in London than Bengal tigers," as he said one day to Mr Stodham: "They ought to have been in the cavalry. But they aren't—curse it—what is to be done? Why could I not breed clerks?" The immediate thing to be done was to light the suspended cigar. It was lucky if the weather just at that time took a fine turn; if Harry and Lewis, for a wonder, were persuaded to spend all day and every day at school; if Mrs Morgan was away in Wales; if Jessie's voice was perfect, singing

"The cuckoo is a merry bird . . ."

I recall such a time. The wall-flower had turned out to be just the mixture of blood colour and lemon that Mr Morgan liked best. The water-lilies were out on the pond. The pigeons lay all along under the roof ridge, too idle to coo except by mistake or in a dream. Jack and Roland were working hard at some machinery in the yard. The right horse, it seems, had won the Derby.

On the evenings in such a season Philip and I had to bring to light the fishing-tackle, bind hooks on gut and gimp, varnish the binding, mix new varnish, fit the rods together, practise casting in the Wilderness, with a view to our next visit, which would be in August, to my aunt Rachel's at Lydiard Constantine. There would be no eggs to be found so late, except a few woodpigeons', linnets', and swallows', but these late finds in the intervals of fishing—when it was too hot, for example—had a special charm. The nuts would be ripe before we left. . . . On these evenings we saw only the fishing things, the Wilderness, and Lydiard Constantine.

This weather was but a temporary cure for Mr Morgan's curiosity as to what Jack and Roland were to do. You could tell that he was glad to see Roland's face again, home from Canada with some wolf skins after a six months' absence; but it was not enough. The fellow had been in an office once for a much shorter period. The one thing to draw him early from bed was hunting. Well, but he was a fine fellow. How should all the good in him be employed? It could not be left to the gods; and yet assuredly the gods would have their way.

Everybody else did something. Aurelius earned a living, though his hands proclaimed him one who was born neither to toil nor spin. Higgs, too, did no one knew what, but something that kept him in tobacco and bowler hats, in the times when he was not fishing in the Wilderness or looking after his pigeons in the yard. For it so happened—and caused nobody surprise—that all the pigeons at Abercorran House were his. Mr Morgan looked with puzzled disapproval from Higgs to Roland and Jack, and back again to Higgs. Higgs had arrived and stayed under their shadow. It was a little mysterious, but so it was, and Mr Morgan could not help seeing and wondering why the two should afflict themselves with patronising one like fat Higgs. Once when Roland struck him, half in play, he bellowed distractedly, not for pain but for pure rabid terror. He went about whistling; for he had a little, hard mouth made on purpose. I thought him cruel, because one day when he saw that, owing to some misapprehension, I was expecting two young pigeons for the price of one, he put the head of one into his mouth and closed his teeth. . . . Whilst I was still silly with disgust and horror he gave me the other bird. But he understood dogs. I have seen Roland listen seriously while Higgs was giving an opinion on some matter concerning Ladas, Bully, Spot, or Granfer; yet Roland was reputed to know all about dogs, and almost all about bitches.

That did not console Mr Morgan. Wherever he looked he saw someone who was perfectly content with Roland and everything else, just as they were, at Abercorran House. Mr Stodham, for example, was all admiration, with a little surprise. Aurelius, again, said that if such a family, house, and backyard, had not existed, they would have to be invented, as other things less pleasant and necessary had been. When rumours were afloat that perhaps Mr Morgan would be compelled to give up the house Aurelius exclaimed: "It is impossible, it is disgraceful. Let the National Gallery go, let the British Museum go, but preserve the Morgans and Abercorran House." Mr Torrance, of course, agreed with Aurelius. He wrote a poem about the house, but, said Aurelius, "It was written with tears for ink, which is barbarous. He has not enough gall to translate tears into good ink." Higgs naturally favoured things as they were, since the yard at Abercorran House was the best possible place for his birds. As for me, I was too young, but Abercorran House made London tolerable and often faultless.

Ann's opinion was expressed in one word: "Wales." She thought that the family ought to go back to Wales, that all would be well there. In fact, she regarded Abercorran House as only a halt, though she admitted that there were unfriendly circumstances. The return to Wales was for her the foundation or the coping stone always. She would not have been greatly put out if there had been a public subscription or grant from the Civil list to make Abercorran House and Mr Morgan, Jessie, Ann herself, Jack, Roland, Philip, Harry, Lewis, Ladas, Bully, Spot, Granfer, the pigeons, the yard, the Wilderness and the jackdaws, the pond and the water-lilies, as far as possible immortal, and a possession for ever, without interference from Board of Works, School Board

inspectors, Rate Collectors, surveyors of taxes, bailiffs and re-
coverers of debts, moreover without any right on the part of the
public to touch this possession except by invitation, with explicit
approval by Roland and the rest. It should have been done. A
branch of the British Museum might have been especially created
to protect this stronghold, as doubtless it would have been protected had it included a dolmen, tumulus, or British camp, or other
relic of familiar type. As it was not done, a bailiff did once share the
kitchen with Ann, a short man completely enveloped in what had
been, at about the time of Albert the Good, a fur-lined overcoat,
and a silk hat suitable for a red Indian. Most of his face was nose,
and his eyes and nose both together looked everlastingly over the
edge of the turned-up coat-collar at the ground. His hands must
have been in his coat-pockets. I speak of his appearance when he
took the air; for I did not see him at Abercorran House. There he
may have produced his hands and removed his hat from his head
and lifted up his eyes from the ground—a thing impossible to his
nose. He may even have spoken—in a voice of ashes. But at least
on the day after his visit all was well at Abercorran House with man
and bird and beast. The jackdaws riding a south-west wind in the
sun said "Jack" over and over again, both singly and in volley.
Only Higgs was disturbed. He, it seems, knew the visitor, and from
that day dated his belief in the perishableness of mortal things, and
a moderated opinion of everything about the Morgans except the
pigeon-house and Roland. Mr Morgan perhaps did not, but
everybody else soon forgot the bailiff. On the day after his visit,
nevertheless, Philip was still indignant. He was telling me about
the battle of Hastings. All I knew and had cared to know was
summed up in the four figures—1066. But Philip, armed with a
long-handled mallet, had constituted himself the English host on
the hill brow, battering the Normans downhill with yells of "Out,
out," and "God Almighty," and also "Out Jew." For his enemy was
William of Normandy and the Jew bailiff in one. With growls of
"Out, out" through foaming set lips, he swung the mallet repeat-
edly, broke a Windsor chair all to pieces, and made the past live
again.

CHAPTER XIX

THE INTERLUDE OF HIGH BOWER

ANN must have had the bailiff's visit in mind when she said, not long after:

"Philip, what would you give to be back, all of you, at Abercorran?"

"Silly," he answered, "I haven't got anything good enough to give, you know. . . . But I would give up going to Our Country for a whole year. I would do anything. . . . But this isn't bad, is it, Arthur?"

Depth of feeling was (to me) so well conveyed by those two mean words that for the life of me I could only corroborate them with a fervent repetition:

"Not bad."

The words expressed, too, a sense of loyalty to the remote idea of Abercorran town itself.

"But High Bower was better, wasn't it," said Ann, to tease him, and to remind him of his duty to the old Abercorran.

"Come on, Arthur," was his reply, "I have got a squirrel to skin."

High Bower was the place in Wiltshire where the Morgan family had paused between Abercorran and London. It was not quite a satisfactory memory to some of them, because there seemed no reason why they should have left Wales if they were going to live in the country; and, then, in a year's time they went to London, after all. Philip never mentioned High Bower, but Mr Stodham knew it—what did he not know in Wiltshire?—and one day he asked me to accompany him on a visit. He had promised to look over the house for a friend.

The village was an archipelago of thatched cottages, sprinkled here and there, and facing all ways, alongside an almost equal

147

number of roads, lanes, tracks, footpaths, and little streams, so numerous and interlaced that they seemed rather to cut it off from the world than to connect it. With much the same materials to use—thatch and brick, thatch and half-timber, or tiles for both roof and walls—the builders of it had made each house different, because thus it had to be, or the man would have it so, or he could not help it, or thus time had decided with the help of alterations and additions. All were on one side of the shallow, flashing river, though it so twined that it appeared to divide some and to surround others, and no bridges were visible. Some of the houses were out in the midst of the mown fields with their troops of tossers, rakers, and pitchforkers, and the high-laden waggons like houses moving. Others were isolated in the sappy, unfooted water-meadows full of tall sedge and iris that hid the hooting moorhen. Remains of the old mill and mill-house, of red, zig-zagged bricks and black timber in stripes, stood apparently on an island, unapproached by road or path, the walls bathed and half-buried in dark humid weeds and the foaming bloom of meadow-sweet. The village had two sounds, the clucking of fowls disturbed from a bath in the road dust, and the gush of the river over an invisible leafy weir, and this was no sound at all, but a variety of silence.

At length I realised that the village was at an end, and before us was a steep, flowery bank, along which at oblivious intervals a train crawled out of beeches, looked a little at the world and entered beeches again, then a tunnel. The train left the quiet quieter, nor did it stop within five miles of High Bower. The railway, which had concentrated upon itself at certain points the dwellings and business of the countryside, left this place, which had resolved to remain where it was, more remote than before.

As we went under the bridge of the embankment I thought we must have missed the Morgans' old house. I wondered if it could have been that last and best farmhouse, heavy and square, that stood back, beyond a green field as level as a pool and three chestnut-trees. Horses were sheltering from the sun under the trees, their heads to the trunks. The cows had gone to the shade of the house, and were all gazing motionless towards the impenetrable gloom of the windows. The barns, sheds, and lodges, were in themselves a village. The last outhouse almost touched the road, a cart-lodge shadowy and empty but for a waggon with low sides curving up forward like the bows of a boat, and itself as delicate as a boat, standing well up on four stout, not ponderous, wheels, and bearing a builder's name from East Stour in Dorset. Now this house and its appurtenances I thought entirely suitable to the Morgans, and my thoughts returned to them as we went under the bridge. Well, and there was the house we were making for, at the foot of the embankment on the other side. It solved a small mystery at once. Our road, before coming to the railway, had cut through a double avenue of limes, which appeared to start at the embankment and terminate a qaurter of a mile away at the top of a gentle rise. They were fine trees, many of them clouded with bunches of mistletoe as big as herons' nests. What was the meaning of the avenue? At neither end was a house to be seen. But, there, at the foot of the embankment, separated from it by two pairs of limes, was the house belonging to the avenue—the Morgans' house, New House by name. The railway had cut through its avenue; a traveller passing could easily have thrown a stone into any one of the chimneys of New House.

A weedy track led out of the road on the right, along under the embankment, up to the house. No smoke rose up from it, not a sound came from the big square windows, or the door between its two pairs of plain stone columns, or the stable on one hand or the garden on the other. The sun poured down on it; it did not respond. It looked almost ugly, a biggish, awkward house, neither native nor old, its walls bare and weathered without being mellowed. In a window, facing anyone who approached it from the road, it announced that it was "To be let or sold" through a firm of solicitors in London. The flower borders were basely neglected, yet not wild. Cows had broken in. . . . It was an obvious stranger, and could only have seemed at home on the main road a little way out of some mean town. It was going to the dogs unlamented.

As we were opening the door a cottage woman attached herself to us, eager, as it proved, to be the first villager to enter since the

Morgans, "the foreigners," had departed. The railway embankment, as she explained, had driven them out, but off the sun, and
kept away new tenants. She left no corner unexplored, sometimes
alleging some kind of service to us, but as a rule out of unashamed
pure delight, talking continually either in comment on what was
there, or to complete the picture of the Morgans, as seen or
invented during those twelve months of their residence.

They were foreigners, she said, who talked and sang in a foreign
language, but could speak English when they wanted to. They
were not rich, never entertained. Such ill-behaved children. . . .
No, there was nothing against them; they didn't owe a penny. . . .
She admired the big rooms downstairs, with pillared doorways and
mantelpieces—they had a dingy palatial air. In the same rooms
with the shiny columns were broad, blackened, open fire-places,
numerous small irregular cupboards, cracked and split. Walls and
doors were undoubtedly marked by arrows and pistol-shot; someone had drawn a target in a corner—"Master Roland," said the
woman. "He was a nice lad, too; or would have been if he had been
English." The spider-webs from wall and ceiling might have been
as old as the house. "The maids had too much to do, playing with
all those children, to keep the place clean. Ignorant those children
were, too. I asked one of the little ones who was the Queen, and he
said 'Gwenny. . . .' I don't know . . . some Jerusalem name that
isn't in the history books. . . . I asked an older one what was the
greatest city in the world, and he said 'Rome.' They were real
gentry, too. But there was something funny about them. One of
them came running into my shop once and said to me, 'I've found
the dragon, Mrs Smith. Come and see—I'll protect you. He has
four horns of ebony, two long and two not so long, and two big
diamond eyes a long way from his horns. He has a neck as thick as
his body, but smooth; his body is like crape. He has no legs, but he
swims over the world like a fish. He is as quiet as an egg.' And he
took me down the road and showed me a black slug such as you
tread on by the hundred without so much as knowing it. They had
no more regard for the truth than if they were lying. . . .

"You never saw the like of them for happiness. When I used to stop at the gate and see them in the grass, perhaps soaking wet, tumbling about and laughing as if they weren't Christians at all, I said to myself: 'Oh, dear, dear me, what trouble there must be in store for those beautiful children, that they should be so happy now. God preserve them, if it be his will.' I whispered: 'Hush, children, be a bit more secret-like about it.' It don't do to boast about anything, let alone happiness. I remember one of them dying sudden. She was little more than a baby; such a child for laughing, as if she was possessed; pretty, too, a regular little moorhen, as you might say, for darkness and prettiness, and fond of the water. I saw one of the maids after the funeral, and took occasion to remark that it was a blessing the child was taken to a better world so soon, before she had known a minute's sorrow. She fired up—she was outlandish, too, as the maids always were, and talked their tongue, and stood up for them as if they were paid for it—and she says, looking that wicked, 'Master says he will never forgive it, and I never will. If she had been a peevish child, I don't say we shouldn't have been wild because she had missed every-thing, but to take away a child like that before she could defend herself is a most unchristian act' . . . and that sort of thing. Oh, there was wickedness in them, though they never wronged any-body."

She pointed to the shot marks in a door, and pronounced that no good could come to a family where the children did such things. At each room she made guesses, amounting often to positive assevera-tion, as to whose it had been. Few enough were the marks of ownership to untutored eyes—chiefly the outlines, like shadows, of furniture and of books that once had leaned against the wall. One door was marked by a series of horizontal lines like those on a thermometer, where children's height had been registered at irregular intervals, the hand or stick pressing down the curls for truth's sake.

Upstairs the passages rambled about as in an old house, and when doors were shut they were dark and cavernous. The rooms themselves were light almost to dazzling after the passages. The light added to their monotony, or what would have been monotony if we had known nothing of their inhabitants. Even so, there were Megan and Ivor whom we had never known. Ivor came between Roland and Philip, "He was the blackest of the black," said Mrs Smith, "brown in the face and black in the hair like a bay horse. He was one for the water; made a vow he would swim from here to the sea, or leastways keep to the water all the way. He got over the second mill-wheel. He swam through the parson's lawn when there was a garden-party. But he had to give up because he kept tasting the water to see how soon it got salt, and so half drowned himself. He came into my shop just as he was born to remind me about the fireworks I had promised to stock for Guy Fawkes day, and that was in September. But he fell out of a tree and was dead before the day came, and, if you will believe me, his brother bought up the fireworks there and then and let them off on the grave."

A wall in one room had on it a map of the neighbourhood, not with the real names, but those of the early kingdoms of England and Wales. The river was the Severn. Their own fields were the land of Gwent. Beyond them lay Mercia and the Hwiccas. The men of Gwent could raid across the Severn, and (in my opinion) were pleased with the obstacle. Later, the projected embankment had been added to the map. This was Offa's Dyke, grimly shutting them out of the kingdoms of the Saxons. I recognised Philip's hand in the work. For his later Saxon fervour was due simply to hate of the Normans: before they came he would have swung his axe as lustily against the Saxons. From this room I could just see the tips of some of the avenue trees beyond the embankment.

We had seen far more of the house than was necessary to decide Mr Stodham against it, when Mrs Smith begged me to stay upstairs a moment while she ran out; she wished me to mark for her a window which she was to point out to me from below. "That's it," she said, after some hesitation, as I appeared at last at the window of a small room looking away from the railway. Nothing in the room distinguished it from the rest save one small black disc with an auburn rim to it on the dark ceiling—one disc only, not, as in the other rooms, several, overlapping, and mingled with traces of the flames of ill-lighted lamps. "Mrs Morgan," I thought at once. Some one evidently had sat long there at a table by night. "I never could make out who it was had this room," said Mrs Smith, coming up breathless: "It used to have a red blind and a lamp always burning. My husband said it did look so cosy; he thought it must be Mr Morgan studying at his books. The milkers saw it in the early morning in winter; they said it was like the big red bottles in a chemist's window. The keeper said you might see it any hour of night. I didn't like it myself. It didn't look to me quite right, like a red eye. You couldn't tell what might be going on behind it, any more than behind a madman's eye. I've thought about it often, trying to picture the inside of that room. My husband would say to me: 'Bessy, the red window at New House did look nice to-night as I came home from market. I'm sure they're reading and stying something larned, astrology or such, behind that red blind.' 'Don't you believe it, James' says I, 'learned it may be, but not *according*. If they want to burn a light all night they could have a black blind. Who else has got a red blind? It isn't fit. I can't think how you bear that naughty red light on a night like this, when there are as many stars in the sky as there are letters in the Bible.' Now, which of them used to sit here? Somebody sat all alone, you may depend upon it, never making a sound nor a stir."

Another room made her think of "Miss Jessie, the one that picked up the fox when he was creeping as slow as slow through their garden, and hid him till the hounds found another fox. . . . Oh, dear, to think what a house this used to be, and so nice and quiet now . . . dreadful quiet. . . . I really must be going, if there is nothing more I can do for you."

Downstairs again the sight of the shot marks in the door set Mrs Smith off again, but in a sobered tone:

"You won't take the house, I'm thinking, sir? No. I wouldn't myself, not for anything. . . . It would be like wearing clothes a person had died in. They never meant us to see these things all in their disabill. 'Tis bad enough to be haunted by the dead, but preserve me from the ghosts of the living. It is more fit for a Hospital, now, or a Home. . . . Those people were like a kind of spirits, like they used to see in olden time. They did not know the sorrow and wickedness of the world as it really is. 'Can the rush grow up without noise? Can the flag grow without water? Whilst it is yet in his greenness, and not cut down, it withereth before any other herb.' Yet you would think they meant to live for ever by the way they went about, young and old. . . . One night I was coming home late and I saw all these windows lit up, every one, and there were people in them all. It was as if the place was a hollow cloud with fire in it and people dancing. Only the red blind was down, and as bright as ever. It called to my mind a story the old Ann used to tell, about a fellow going home from a fair and seeing a grand, gorgeous house close by the road, and lovely people dancing and musicking in it, where there hadn't been a house before of any kind. He went in and joined them and slept in a soft warm bed, but in the morning he woke up under a hedge. I sort of expected to see there wasn't any house there next morning, it looked *that strange*."

While we were having tea in her parlour Mrs Smith showed us a photograph of "Miss Megan," an elder sister of Jack and Roland, whom I had never heard of, nor I think had Mr Stodham. I shall not forget the face. She was past twenty, but clearly a fairy child, one who, like the flying Nicolete, would be taken for a fay by the woodfolk (and they should know). Her dark face was thin and shaped like a wedge, with large eyes generous and passionate under eyebrows that gave them an apprehensive expression, though the fine clear lips could not have known fear or any other sort of control except pity. The face was peering through chestnut leaves, looking as soft as a hare, but with a wildness like the hare's which, when it is in peril, is almost terrible. I think it was a face destined to be loved often, but never to love, or but once. It could draw men's lips and pens, and would fly from them and refuse to be entangled in any net of words or kisses. It would fly to the high, solitary places, and its lovers would cry out: "Oh, delicate bird, singing in the prickly furze, you are foolish, too, or why will you not come down to me where the valleys are pleasant, where the towns are, and everything can be made according to your desire?" Assuredly, those eyes were for a liberty not to be found among men, but only

154

among the leaves, in the clouds, or on the waves, though fate might confine them in the labyrinth of a city. But not a word of her could I learn except once when I asked Ann straight out. All she said was: "God have mercy on Megan."

Two years after our visit the New House was taken by a charitable lady as a school and home for orphans. In less than a year she abandoned it, and within a year after that, it was burnt to the ground. The fields of Gwent and the lime avenue may still be seen by railway travellers. Gypsies have broken the hedges and pitched their tents unforbidden. All kinds of people come in December for the mistletoe. The place is utterly neglected, at least by the living.

On the whole, I think, Mr Stodham and I were both sorry for our day at High Bower. It created a suspicion—not a lasting one with me—that Abercorran House would not endure for ever. Mr Stodham's account made Mr Torrance look grave, and I understood that he wrote a poem about New House. Higgs remarked that if the Morgans had stayed at High Bower he could not imagine what he should have done with his pigeons. Aurelius enjoyed every detail, from the map to Megan's photograph. Aurelius had no acquaintance with regret or envy. He was glad of Mr Stodham's account of New House, and glad of Abercorran House in reality. He was one that sat in the sunniest places (unless he was keeping Jessie out) all day, and though he did not despise the moon he held the fire at Abercorran House a more stable benefactor. Neither sun nor moon made him think of the day after to-morrow, and to-morrow, and to-morrow. "Aurelius," said Mr Morgan, "is the wisest man out of Christendom and therefore the wisest of all men. He knows that England in the nineteenth century does not allow any but a working man to die of starvation unless he wants to. Aurelius is not a working man, nor does he desire to starve. He is not for an age, but for to-day."

CHAPTER XX

THE perfume of the fur of the squirrel we skinned on that January evening—when Ann teased Philip about High Bower—I well remember. I liked it then; now I like it the more for every year which has since gone by. It was one of the years when I kept a diary, and day by day I can trace its seasons. The old year ended in frost and snow. The new year began with thaw, and with a postal order from my aunt at Lydiard Constantine, and the purchase of three yards of cotton wool in readiness for the nesting season and our toll of eggs. On the next day snow fell again, in the evening the streets were ice, and at Abercorran House Philip and I made another drawer of a cabinet for birds' eggs. Frost and snow continued on the morrow, compelling us to make a sledge instead of a drawer for the cabinet. The sledge carried Philip and me alternately throughout the following day, over frozen roads and footpaths. The fifth day was marked by a letter from Lydiard Constantine, eighteen degrees of frost, and more sledging with Philip, and some kind of attention (that has left not a wrack behind) to Sallust's "Catiline" . . .

Within a fortnight the pigeons were beginning to lay, and as one of the nests contained the four useless eggs of an imbecile pair of hens, we tasted thus early the pleasure of blowing one egg in the orthodox manner and sucking three. This being Septuagesima Sunday, nothing would satisfy us but an immediate visit to Our Country, where the jays' nests and others we had robbed seven months before were found with a thrill all but equal to that of May, and always strictly examined in case of accidents or miracles. For there had now been a whole week of spring sun shining on our hearts, and on the plumage of the cock pheasant we stalked in vain. The thrush sang. The blackbird sang. With the Conversion of St Paul came rain, and moreover school, Thucydides,

Shakespeare's "Richard the Second," and other unrealities and afflictions, wherein I had to prove again how vain it is "to cloy the hungry edge of appetite by bare imagination of a feast" at old Gaunt's command. But Quinquagesima Sunday meant rising in the dark and going out with Philip, to watch the jays, always ten yards ahead of our most stealthy stepping—to climb after old woodpigeons' nests, to cut hazel sticks, to the tune of many skylarks. Alas, a sprained foot could not save me from school on Monday. But now the wild pigeons dwelling about the school began to coo all day long and to carry sticks for their nests. Out on the football field, in the bright pale light and the south-west wind the black rooks courted—and more; the jackdaws who generally accompanied them were absent somewhere. What then mattered it whether Henri Quatre or Louis Quatorze were the greatest of the Bourbon kings, as some of my school-fellows debated? Besides, when February was only half through, Aunt Rachel formally invited Philip and me to Lydiard Constantine for Easter. This broke the winter's back. Frost and fog and Bright's "History of England" were impotent. We began to write letters to the chosen three or four boys at Lydiard Constantine. We made, in the gas jets at Abercorran House, tubes of glass for the sucking of bird's eggs. We bought egg drills. We made egg-drills for ourselves. . . . The cat had kittens. One pair of Higgs' pigeons hatched out their eggs. The house-sparrows were building. The almond-trees blossomed in the gardens of "Brockenhurst" and the other houses. The rooks now stayed in the football field until five. The larks sang all day, invisible in the strong sun and burning sky. The gorse was a bonfire of bloom. Then, at last, on St David's day, the rooks were building, the woodpigeons cooing on every hand, the first lambs were heard.

Day after day left us indignant that, in spite of all temptations, no thrush or blackbird had laid an egg, so far as we knew. But all things seemed possible. One day, in a mere afternoon walk, we found, not far beyond a muddle of new streets, a district "very beautiful and quiet", says the diary. Losing our way, we had to hire a punt to take us across the stream—I suppose, the Wandle. Beautiful and quiet, too, was the night when Philip scaled the high

railings into the grounds of a neighbouring institution, climbed
one of the tall elms of its rookery—I could see him up against the
sky, bigger than any of the nests, in the topmost boughs—and
brought down the first egg. It was the Tuesday before an early
Easter, a clear blue, soft day which drove clean out of our minds all
thought of fog, frost, and rain, past or to come. Mr Stodham had
come into the yard of Abercorran House on the way to his office, as
I had on my way to school. Finding Aurelius sitting in the sun with
Ladas, he said in his genial, nervous way: "That's right. You are
making the best of a fine day. Goodness knows what it will be like
to-morrow." "And Goodness cares," said Aurelius, almost angrily,
"I don't." "Sorry, sorry," said Mr Stodham, hastily lighting his
pipe. "All right," said Aurelius, "but if you care about to-morrow, I
don't believe you really care about to-day. You are one of those
people, who say that if it is not always fine, or fine when they want
it, they don't care if it is never fine, and be damned to it, say they.
And yet they don't like bad weather so well as I do, or as Jessie does.
Now, rain, when it ought not to be raining, makes Jessie angry,
and if the day were a man or woman she would come to terms with
it, but it isn't, and what is more, Jessie rapidly gets sick of being
angry, and as likely as not she sings 'Blow away the morning dew,'
and finds that she likes the rain. She has been listening to the talk
about rain by persons who want to save Day and Martin. I prefer
Betty Martin. . . . Do you know, Arthur tells me the house
martins will soon be here?" We looked up together to see if it was a
martin that both of us had heard, or seemed to hear, overhead, but,
if it was, it was invisible.

Every year such days came—any time in Lent, or even before. I
take it for granted that, as an historical fact, they were followed, as
they have been in the twentieth century, by fog, frost, mists,
drizzle, rain, sleet, snow east wind, and north wind, and I know
very well that we resented these things. But we loved the sun. We
strove to it in imagination through the bad weather, believing in
every kind of illusory hint that the rain was going to stop, and so
on. Moreover rain had its merits. For example, on a Sunday, it
kept the roads nearly as quiet as on a week day, and we could have

Our Country, or Richmond Park, or Wimbledon Common, all to ourselves. Then, again, what a thing it was to return wet, with a rainy brightness in your eyes, to change rapidly, to run round to Abercorran House, and find Philip and Ann expecting you in the kitchen, with a gooseberry tart, currant tart, raspberry tart, plum tart, blackberry tart, cranberry and apple tart, apple tart, according to season; and mere jam or syrup tart in the blank periods. My love of mud also I trace to that age, because Philip and I could escape all company by turning out of a first class road into the black mash of a lane. If we met anyone there, it was a carter contending with the mud, a tramp sitting between the bank and a fire, or a filthy bird-catcher beyond the hedge.

If the lane was both muddy and new to us, and we two, Philip and I, turned into it, there was nothing which we should have thought out of its power to present in half a mile or so, nothing which it would have overmuch astonished us by presenting. It might have been a Gypsy camp, it might have been the terrestrial Paradise of Sheddad the son of Ad—we should have fitted either into our scheme of the universe. Not that we were *blasé*; for every new thrush's egg in the season had a new charm for us. Not that we had been flightily corrupted by fairy tales and marvels. No: the reason was that we only regarded as impossible such things as a score of 2000 in first class cricket, an air ship, or the like; and the class of improbabilities did not exist for us. Nor was this all. We were not merely ready to welcome strange things when we had walked half a mile up a lane and met no man, but we were in a gracious condition for receiving whatever might fall to us. We did not go in search of miracles, we invited them to come to us. What was familiar to others was never, on that account, tedious or contemptible to us. I remember that when Philip and I first made our way through London to a shop which was depicted in an advertisement, in spite of the crowds on either hand all along our route, in spite of the full directions of our elders, we were as much elated by our achievement as if it had been an arduous discovery made after a journey in a desert. In our elation there was some suspicion that our experience had been secret, adventurous, and unique. As to the crowd, we glided through it as angels might. This building, expected by us and known to all, astonished us as much as the walls of Sheddad the son of Ad unexpectedly towering would have done.

Sometimes in our rare London travels we had a glimpse of a side street, a row of silent houses all combined as it were into one grey palace, a dark doorway, a gorgeous window, a surprising man disappearing. . . . We looked, and though we never said so, we believed that we alone had seen these things, that they had never been seen before. We should not have expected to see them there if we went again. Many and many a time have we looked, have I alone in more recent years looked, for certain things thus revealed to us in passing. Either it happened that the thing was different from what it had once been, or it had disappeared altogether.

Now and then venturing down a few side streets where the system was rectangular and incapable of deceiving, we came on a church full of sound or gloomily silent—I do not know how to describe the mingled calm and pride in the minds of the discoverers. Some of the very quiet, apparently uninhabited courts, for example, made us feel that corners of London had been deserted and forgotten, that anyone could hide away there, living in secrecy as in a grave. Knowing how we ourselves, walking or talking together, grew oblivious of all things that were not within our brains, or vividly and desirably before our eyes, feeling ourselves isolated in proud delight, deserted and forgotten of the multitude who were not us, we imagined, I suppose, that houses and other things could have a similar experience, or could share it with us, were we to seek refuge there like Morgan in his mountain tower. The crowd passing and surrounding us consisted of beings unlike us, incapable of our isolation or delight: the retired houses whispering in quiet alleys must be the haunt of spirits unlike the crowd and more like us, or, if not, at least they must be waiting in readiness for such. I recognised in them something that linked them to Abercorran House and distinguished them from Brockenhurst.

Had these favoured houses been outwardly as remarkable as they were in spirit they might have pleased us more, but I am not certain. Philip had his house with the windows that were as the days of the year. But I came only once near to seeing, with outward eyes, such a house as perhaps we desired without knowing it. Suddenly, over the tops of the third or fourth and final ridge of roofs, visible a quarter of a mile away from one of the windows at Abercorran House, much taller than any of the throng of houses and clear in the sky over them, I saw a castle on a high rock. It resembled St Michael's Mount, only the rock was giddier and had a narrower summit, and the castle's three clustered round towers of unequal height stood up above it like three fingers above a hand. When I pointed it out to Philip he gave one dark, rapid glance as of mysterious understanding, and looked at me, saying slowly:

> " 'A portal as of shadowy adamant
>   Stands yawning on the highway of the life
> Which we all tread, a cavern huge and gaunt;
>   Around it rages an unceasing strife
> Of shadows, like the restless clouds that haunt
> The gap of some cleft mountain, lifted high
> Into the whirlwind of the upper sky.
> And many pass it by with careless tread,
> Not knowing that a shadowy. . . .'

A shadowy *what*, Arthur? At any rate that is the place.'

In those days, Philip was beginning to love Shelley more than he loved Aurelius or me.

I had not seen that pile before. With little trouble I could have located it almost exactly: I might have known that the particular street had no room for a sublimer St Michael's Mount. If we passed the spot during the next few days we made no use of the evidence against the tower, which satisfied us in varying degrees until in process of time it took its place among the other chimney clusters of our horizon. It was not disillusioned as to this piece of fancy's architecture, nor was I thereafter any more inclined to take a surveyor's view of the surface of the earth. Stranger things, probably, than St Michael's Mount have been thought and done in that street: we did not know it, but our eyes accepted this symbol of them with gladness, as in the course of nature. Not much less fantastic was our world than the one called up by lights seen far off before a traveller in a foreign and a dark, wild land.

Therefore Spring at Lydiard Constantine was to Philip and me more than a portion of a regular renascence of Nature. It was not an old country marvellously at length arraying itself after an old custom, but an invasion of the old as violent as our suburban St Michael's Mount. It was as if the black, old, silent earth had begun to sing as sweet as when Jessie sang unexpectedly "Blow away the morning dew." It was not a laborious, orderly transformation, but a wild, divine caprice. We supposed that it would endure for ever, though it might (as I see now) have turned in one night to Winter. But it did not.

That Spring was a poet's Spring. "Remember this Spring," wrote Aurelius in a letter, "then you will know what a poet means when he says *Spring*." Mr Stodham, who was not a poet, but wrote verse passionately, was bewildered by it, and could no longer be kept from exposing his lines. He called the Spring both fiercely joyous, and melancholy. He addressed it as a girl, and sometimes as a thousand gods. He said that it was as young as the dew-drop freshly globed on the grass tip, and also as old as the wind. He proclaimed that it had conquered the earth, and that it was as fleeting as a poppy. He praised it as golden, as azure, as green, as snow-white, as chill and balmy, as bright and dim, as swift and languid, as kindly and cruel, as true and fickle. Yet he certainly told an infinitely small part of the truth concerning that Spring. It is memorable to me chiefly on account of a great poet.

For a day or two, at Lydiard Constantine, Philip roamed with me up and down hedgerows, through copses, around pools, as he had done in other Aprils, but though he found many nests he took not one egg, not even a thrush's egg that was pure white and would have been unique in his collection, or in mine; neither was I allowed to take it. Moreover, after the first two or three days he only came reluctantly—found hardly any nests—quarrelled furiously with the most faithful of the Lydiard boys for killing a thrush (though it was a good shot) with a catapult. He now went about muttering unintelligible things in a voice like a clergyman. He pushed through a copse saying magnificently:

"Unfathomable sea whose waves are years."

He answered an ordinary question by Aunt Rachel with:

"Away, away, from men and towns,
To the wild wood and the downs."

Tears stood in his eyes while he exclaimed:

"Grief made the young Spring wild, and she threw down
Her kindling buds, as if she Autumn were,
Or they dead leaves."

Like a somnambulist he paced along, chanting:

"Earth, Ocean, Air, beloved brotherhood. . . ."

The sight of a solitary cottage would draw from him those lines beginning:

"A portal as of shadowy adamant. . . ."

Over and over again, in a voice somewhere between that of Irving and a sheep, he repeated:

"From what Hyrcanian glen or frozen hill,
Or piny promontory of the Arctic main,
Or utmost islet inaccessible. . . ."

With a frenzy as of one who suffered wounds, insults, hunger and thirst and pecuniary loss, for Liberty's sweet sake, he cried out to the myriad emerald leaves:

"Oh, that the wise from their bright minds would kindle

> Such lamps within the dome of this dim world,
> That the pale name of *Priest* might shrink and dwindle
> Into the *Hell* from which it first was hurled. . . ."

He used to say to me, falling from the heights of recitation:

"Shelley lived in the time of the Duke of Wellington. He was the son of a rich old baronet in Sussex, but he had nothing to do with his parents as soon as he could escape from them. He wrote the greatest lyrics that ever were—that is, songs not meant to be sung, and no musician could write good enough music for them, either. He was tall, and brave, and gentle. He feared no man, and he almost loved death. He was beautiful. His hair was long, and curled, and had been nearly black, but it was going grey when he died. He was drowned in the Mediterranean at thirty. The other poets burnt his body on the sea-shore, but one of them saved the heart and buried it at Rome with the words on the stone above it, *Cor cordium*, Heart of hearts. It is not right, it is not right. . . ."

He would mutter, "It is not right," but what he meant I could not tell, unless he was thus—seventy years late—impatiently indignant at the passing of Shelley out of this earth. As likely as not he would forget his indignation, if such it was, by whispering—but not to me—with honied milky accents, as of one whose feet would refuse to crush a toad or bruise a flower:

> "Thou Friend, whose presence on my wintry heart
>   Fell like bright Spring upon some herbless plain,
> How beautiful and calm and free thou wert
>   In thy young wisdom, when the mortal chain
>   Of custom thou didst burst and rend in twain,
> And walk as free as light the clouds among,
>   Which many an envious slave then breath'd in vain
> From his dim dungeon, and my spirit sprung
> To meet thee from the woes which had begirt it long. . . ."

From Philip's tone as he continued the poem, it might have been supposed that he, too, had a young and unloved wife, a rebellious father, a sweet-heart ready to fly with him in the manner suggested by some other lines which he uttered with conviction:

> "A ship is floating in the harbour now,
> A wind is hovering o'er the mountain's brow;
> There is a path on the sea's azure floor,
> No keel has ever ploughed the path before;
> The halcyons brood around the foamless isles;
> The treacherous ocean has forsworn its wiles;
> The merry mariners are bold and free:
> Say, my heart's sister, wilt thou sail with me?"

I have beside me the book which taught Philip this sad bliss, this wild wisdom. The fly-leaves are entirely covered by copies in his hand-writing of the best-loved poems and passages. Between some pages are still the scentless skeletons of flowers and leaves—still more pages bear the stains left by other flowers and leaves—plucked in that spring at Lydiard Constantine. The gilding of the covers for the most part is worn smoothly out; the edges are frayed, the corners broken. Thus the book seems less the work of Shelley than of Philip. It embalms that Spring. Yet why do I say embalmed? It is not dead. It lives while I live and can respond to the incantation of one of the poems in this little book, beginning:

> "Life of Life, thy lips enkindle,
> With their love the breath between them. . . ."

When I first heard them from Philip, Spring was thronging the land with delicious odours, colours, and sounds. I knew how nothing came, yet it was a sweet and natural coming rather than magic—a term then of too narrow application. As nearly as possible I step back those twenty years, and see the beech leaves under the white clouds in the blue and hear the wood wren amongst them, whenever by some chance or necessity I meet that incantation: "Life of Life, thy lips enkindle," and I do not understand them any more than I do the Spring. Both have the power of magic. . . .

165

Not magical, but enchanted away from solidity, seems now that life at Abercorran House, where Jessie, Ann, Aurelius, and the rest, and the dogs, and the pigeons, sat or played in the sun, I suppose, without us and Shelley, throughout that April. There never was again such another Spring, because those that followed lacked Philip. He fell ill and stayed on at Lydiard Constantine to be nursed by my Aunt Rachel, while I went back to read about the Hanseatic League, Clodia (the Lesbia of Catullus), and other phantoms that had for me no existence except in certain printed pages which I would gladly have abolished. With Philip I might have come to care about the Hansa, and undoubtedly about Clodia; but before I had done with them, before the cuckoos of that poet's Spring were silent, he was buried at Lydiard Constantine.

At this point the people at Abercorran House—even Jessie and Aurelius—and the dogs that stretched out in deathlike blessedness under the sun, and the pigeons that courted and were courted in the yard and on the roof, all suddenly retreat from me when I come to that Spring in memory; a haze of ghostly, shimmering silver veils them; without Philip they are as people in a story whose existence I cannot prove. The very house has gone. The elms of the Wilderness have made coffins, if they were not too old. Where is the pond and its lilies? They are no dimmer than the spirits of men and children. But there is always Ann. When "Life of Life" is eclipsed and Spring forgotten, Ann is still in Abercorran Street. I do not think she sees those dim hazed spirits of men and children, dogs and pigeons. Jessie, she tells me, is now a great lady, but rides like the wind. Roland never leaves Caermarthenshire except after a fox. Jack has gone to Canada and will stay. Lewis is something on a ship. Harry owns sheep by thousands, and rents a mighty mountain, and has as many sons as brothers, and the same number of daughters, who have come to the point of resembling Jessie: so says Ann, who has a hundred photographs. Mr Morgan is back at Abercorran. When good fortune returned to the Morgans the whole family went there for a time, leaving Ann behind until the house should be let. She stayed a year. The family began to recover in the country, and to scatter. Jessie married and Jack left England within the year. Ann became a housekeeper first to the new tenant of Abercorran House, afterwards to Mr Jones at Abercorran Street. Otherwise I should not have written down these memories of the Morgans and their friends, men, dogs, and pigeons, and of the sunshine caught by the yard of Abercorran House in those days, and of Our Country, and of that Spring and the "Life of Life" which live, and can only perish, together. Ann says there is another world. "Not a better," she adds firmly. "It would be blasphemous to suppose that God ever made any but the best of worlds—not a better, but a different one, suitable for different people than we are now, you understand, not better, for that is impossible, say I, who have lived in Abercorran—town, house, and street—these sixty years—there is not a better world."

ALSO AVAILABLE IN BOOKMASTERS

THE STORY OF MY LIFE

Ellen Terry

Ellen Terry (1847–1928) was the most magical figure of the Victorian stage, and her enchanting memoirs were described by Ian McKellen recently on Radio 3 as 'the best theatrical autobiography I've ever read.' She wrote these memoirs in 1908, at the end of her main stage career, though her last stage appearance was in 1925. She tells her story very simply and unaffectedly, beginning with her childhood as a travelling player (she first appeared on stage at the age of nine), her ill-fated marriage to the painter G.F. Watts when she was sixteen, her return to the stage and to a series of triumphant successes in London and New York, particularly during her time at the Lyceum with Henry Irving. Her wry and humorous self-portrait is matched by vivid sketches of the great actors and actresses she worked with, and her character study of Irving himself, spendthrift and prodigious in all he did, is in itself enough to ensure the book's place among the classics of the theatre.

240pp, 216 x 135mm, ISBN 0 85115 204 X

THE HOLE IN THE WALL

Arthur Morrison

The Hole in the Wall is one of the most gripping adventure stories ever written. From its unforgetable opening – 'My grandfather was a publican and a sinner, as you will see. His public house was the Hole in the Wall, on the river's edge at Wapping; and his sins – all of them that I know of – are recorded in these pages' – it is a book that you genuinely cannot put down. Stephen Kemp goes to live with his mysterious grandfather after his mother's death, and is gradually drawn into the seedy world which Captain Nat Kemp inhabits, but of which he is determined Stephen shall not become part. Morrison brilliantly conveys the child's sharp observation of all that goes on around him, and builds up a portrait of the East End he himself may have known as a boy; and against this background of dockside life, he unfolds his story in masterly fashion.

179pp, 216 x 135mm, ISBN 0 85115 205 8

THE GREEN HAT

Michael Arlen

The Green Hat is the quintessence of the 'twenties: gay, stylish, mannered and bitter-sweet, a brilliant mixture of cynicism and sentiment. When it first appeared in 1924, it was (as Margaret Bellasis said in *The Dictionary of National Biography*) 'acclaimed, attacked, parodied and read, to the most fabulous degree of best-sellerdom ...' The character of the heroine, Iris Storm, that wanton of quality, "shameless, shameful lady", gallantly crashing to her death in her great yellow Hispano-Suiza – "for Purity" – set a new fashion in fatal charmers: and the pictures of London cafè society were exact as glossy photographs.' Michael Arlen was Armenian by birth, but he was educated in England and was thus entirely at home in English society and yet distanced enough from it to write about it accurately and mockingly, with that brilliance and wit which the English are always supposed to permit to foreigners but to decry in their fellow countrymen. *The Green Hat* is above all a witty tragi-comedy of manners that captures the spirit of the glittering, colourful, yet slightly unreal world of London after the First World War.

Michael Arlen was born in 1895 in Bulgaria. He changed his name from Dikram Kouyoumdjian in 1922 when he became a naturalised British citizen, having already published novels and short stories under his new name. Following the success of *The Green Hat* he wrote a number of further novels, the last of which appeared in 1939. He died in New York in 1956.

244pp, 192 x 129mm, ISBN 0 85115 210 4

THE YELLOW BOOK

The Yellow Book is the most famous of the literary magazines of the 1890s, summing up the mood of those years, when aesthetics became a subject for fierce debate, satirized by *Punch* and by W.S. Gilbert, and as fiercely defended by the artists and writers who formed the new movement. *The Yellow Book*, in its brief three years of existence, came in for more than its fair share of denunciation and derision, particularly for its illustrations by Aubrey Beardsley. Fraser Harrison's selection allows us to find out what all the fuss was about, and he contributes an introduction on the history of the magazine and its social and artistic context. His essay and the selection of contents, by authors and artists who are now deservedly famous, show that *The Yellow Book* was not merely a *succes de scandale*, but still has much to offer us today.

288pp, 216 x 135mm, ISBN 0 85115 207 4